MW01193725

SIZZLE

A MacKenzie Security Novel

LILIANA HART

ISBN: 1494763281
ISBN-13: 978-1494763282

DEDICATION

To all the men and women who serve our country.
Thank you.

CONTENTS

ACKNOWLEDGMENTS

Thanks to Heather, Nicole, Jaye, Molly, and Judy for pulling me back from the ledge while writing this book and assuring me that it was possible to have hot sex in Alaska, even though the suggestions included igloos, dead moose, and using the pee flaps on long johns effectively. I love laughing every day with you.

Thanks to the ladies of The Indie Voice for their unwavering support. I needed it.

Thanks to my reps at iBooks and Amazon who listened patiently while I described the problems of trying to get my characters to have hot sex in Alaska. You all have a lot of patience and a great sense of humor. And you've learned not to panic every time I open my mouth. I appreciate that.

And thanks to all the readers who love the Mackenzies and keep asking, "Where's Shane's story?"

I promise, it's coming.

PROLOGUE

Lyon, France

Three years ago

She'd broken all the rules. But boy, had it been worth it.

Audrey Sharpe tried to open her eyes, but they only fluttered before closing again. The effort was too much. Maybe she'd just stay like this forever—her heart pounding, the sweat cooling on her skin, and the weight of a very attractive man pressing her into the mattress.

"I don't think I can move," Jonah Salt murmured against her neck.

"I'm not complaining. I can't feel my legs anyway." Her eyes slowly opened and she noticed some of the candles had guttered out, so the room was cast in shadow instead of a soft yellow glow.

Jonah had been her partner and trainer for the last eight months. And as of tonight, he was her lover. They were covert agents for Oblivion, an off the books division of the CIA, and they'd just finished a mission they'd been working for months. It hadn't exactly gone as planned, and now they were waiting to tie up a few loose ends and see what their debriefing orders were.

The small chateau that had been turned into a boutique hotel was where they'd planned to regroup if the mission was compromised. It was high traffic and touristy, and no one would ever suspect that they were anything other than a normal couple. It was an act they'd perfected dozens of times before.

But this time had been different. Between the leftover adrenaline rush and the king size bed that dominated the room, it had only taken one look for the sexual tension to crackle between them. It had been a race to the finish after that. But she didn't regret her actions.

Something had been building between them for weeks, though Audrey could admit she'd been attracted to him since he'd been assigned as her trainer. There was something about the sheer maleness of him that had drawn her in like a moth to flame. Jonah hadn't been quite so quick to accept *her* though.

Audrey knew her looks made people underestimate her ability, and she accepted her beauty as a tool—a weapon just as deadly as the knife she perpetually wore in her boot. But others, especially men in this business, didn't trust her beauty, thinking there was nothing beneath the surface. So she had to continually prove herself and her abilities, and be better than they were. Jonah had been wary to take her on. But she soon proved her looks were nothing more than a distraction to hide the killer she was beneath.

She'd been Israeli Mossad—one of the elite *Kidon* assassins—before she'd been captured and tortured by the Syrians. All Mossad agents were trained to withstand various torture techniques, and though the training wasn't pleasant, it had kept her from spilling secrets that would have betrayed her country.

U.S. intelligence agents had rescued her. And she'd been given a choice once she'd been debriefed and made contact with her superiors. She was deemed ineffective by the *Kidon* since she'd been captured, and she had no wish to be one of the numerous intelligence gatherers who did nothing but stare at a computer screen all day. She belonged in the field. So she'd taken the offer the U.S. had given her. A new identity. A new country. A new team.

She'd had no family left in Israel, and though her loyalty had always been to her homeland, she felt the move to the United States was the best she could have made. Her two home countries were allies, and she would defend her new country with honor, just as she had her last.

Her cell phone buzzed—an insistent hum that droned on and on—from the little table across the room. But she was in no hurry to go back to the real world.

"You need to get that?" Jonah asked, kissing the side of her neck before rolling to the other side of the bed. He sat up and ran his fingers through tousled blonde hair in need of a trim.

"That's my private line, so no. Not until tomorrow. I've got the satellite phone if the agency needs to get in touch."

He stood without any self-consciousness at all, and she watched in pure female appreciation as the muscles in his back and buttocks flexed as he stretched. Jonah was an interesting man. Quiet in a lot of ways. But she felt like she'd come to know him well over the last eight months. He was fourteen years older than her own twenty-seven years, and what they said about older men being excellent lovers was true. He knew exactly what he was doing, where to touch and taste to make her blood sing.

His face was an interesting one rather than handsome. The lines that fanned from his eyes and the corners of his mouth were deep, and his beard was flecked with the occasional strand of white. But it was his eyes she'd first noticed. They were the most beautiful shade of blue. She wasn't even sure blue was the correct color to describe them. Streaks of silver shot through them and the iris was ringed by a dark navy. She'd seen them turn cold and implacable as a glacier when they were on the job. And she'd seen them melt to the color of a summer lake only moments ago.

"We've got an early morning tomorrow. The boat will be here to pick us up for debriefing."

Audrey sighed and pulled the covers over her chilled skin. "My favorite part. They're going to be pissed we didn't get the identity of *Proteus*. Francois Renard was the only person we've been able to find who's had direct contact with him. I still don't understand how they got the explosives in. He was right there under surveillance and no one saw anyone go in or out. We're going to take the rap for that."

"Maybe a slap on the knuckles. But it wasn't our job to keep Renard alive. It was our job to get him out. Those explosives were well placed and well timed. We're lucky to be alive. In fact, I'm going to be feeling the aches and pains of this mission for a while." He rubbed his hand over the growth of beard on his face and turned to give her a wry smile. "Field work gets harder as you get older."

"If it makes you feel better, I wrenched my knee when we jumped into that drainage ditch."

His eyebrows raised in surprise. "You should have said something. I would have been… gentler." His mouth quirked and she snorted out a laugh. He could always make her laugh.

"Endorphins make an excellent pain killer."

"Hmm, good point. Don't feel bad about losing Renard. We'll find out who *Proteus* is sooner or later. He's on every worldwide agency's watch list."

Audrey licked her lips and debated whether or not to pass along the information she had. He was her partner. Now her lover. And it wasn't that she didn't trust him. She trusted him with her life. But her Mossad training ran deep, and she wasn't used to sharing viable information. She wasn't used to having a partner, period.

Before she could change her mind, she decided to tell him what she'd learned. "I've got a contact from back home. He thinks he's got a line on the identity of *Proteus,* and I've been waiting for him to get in touch."

"How did he get close enough to get an identity? Can your informant be trusted?"

"Shai isn't Mossad, but he works special assignments on occasion for the Israeli government as a contractor. He told me he set a trap for *Proteus.* You know how we have that partial recording of *Proteus's* voice talking to Renard?"

"Right, but the voice was distorted."

"Shai is a genius with computers. He didn't care about the voice. He wanted to use the partial set of numbers *Proteus* gave to Renard for payment. Shai was able to use those numbers to find the account. And from there he said it was simple to lay a trap. The next time *Proteus* gets online, Shai will have his identity."

"Very clever of your friend. Good work," he nodded approvingly.

"You're not angry at me for keeping it from you?"

"Not at all, love. We all have secrets. Secrets are our line of business. But I'm glad you trusted me enough to tell me. You and I are going to be a hell of a team." He came toward her and ran his finger down the gentle slope of her jawline. "I wanted you from the moment I saw you."

"Liar," she said, laughing. "You told me I wouldn't last two days under your training. I believe you also told me there was no place for beauty queens in espionage. I was never a beauty queen, by the way."

"You and that damn memory of yours. You never forget anything," he said, grinning. "And it looks like I was wrong. You lasted more than two days. Now I can't imagine my life without you in it."

He leaned down and kissed her softly and she felt her heart sigh. This man could make her love him. She was already half way there. And that was something she'd need to think about. She'd never been in love before, and the feeling was both euphoric and terrifying at the same time.

"I'm going to get in the shower. Care to join me?"

"As tempting as that is, I'm not moving from this spot until morning. I'm exhausted. And I'm not sure my legs are ready for walking."

He kissed her again and moved toward the bathroom. "You do excellent things for a man's ego, love. When should your friend have a lockdown on *Proteus*?"

"The last I heard from him was the day before we went in for Renard. He said he thought he'd have it within forty-eight hours."

"Excellent. You sure you don't want to join me? I'm feeling very…rejuvenated all of a sudden."

"Yes, I can see that," she said, laughing again. "Why don't you come back here instead?"

"You're a temptress, Agent Sharpe. But I'm made of stronger stuff than that."

He closed the bathroom door behind him, and Audrey snuggled down in the covers as the shower turned on. She smiled as she heard him whistling. The man loved to whistle, especially while they were prepping for a job. It was his thinking mechanism, and she knew once he started whistling she needed to be quiet and let him ponder through possibilities. It was just one of the quirks they'd learned about each other over their time together.

Wasn't that what love was? Learning each other's idiosyncrasies—likes and dislikes—how to read each other so you knew what your partner wanted without him having to ask?

God. Maybe she was already in love with him. Her phone buzzed again, but her realization kept her immobilized. *Love.* She never thought a relationship would be something she could have. She'd been trained from her twelfth year for Mossad, and then at eighteen she'd been selected for the elite *Kidon.* She'd known nothing else. Her future had been determined for her, and she'd always accepted it as it was.

But Jonah Salt had taken what she'd known and turned it upside down. He'd been her trainer, her friend, and her lover. And she *loved* him. The question of the hour was whether or not he loved her too.

She blew out a shaky breath at that thought and told herself to relax as the shower turned off. Jonah was excellent at reading people. If she wasn't careful he'd know her feelings, and if he didn't feel the same, that could ruin their partnership. They were already breaking agency rules by being involved. They'd be reprimanded and reassigned to different partners in a heartbeat if their sexual relationship was discovered.

Discretion was key—both their outward relationship as well as her personal feelings. Her training had been ingrained and extensive. She could keep her emotions to herself—she'd never cried out once when she'd been tortured by her Syrian captors. And she'd carry the scars on her back and torso forever. But they certainly hadn't bothered Jonah. He had his own share of scars. The scars were just part of who he was, just as hers were part of who she was.

She propped up on her elbow when he came out of the bathroom. A towel was slung low on his hips and droplets of water clung to his skin. He'd shaved and his hair was slicked back from his face.

"It's dangerous to keep looking at me like that, love."

"It's dangerous to make threats if you don't intend to follow through," she said, her voice low and seductive. She pulled back the sheet and her blood pounded faster as his eyes darkened with desire.

Her phone buzzed again and he moved to the table, distracted by the interruption. She could tell by the short length of the buzz that it was a text message instead of a call.

"Can you toss that to me?" she said. "I guess they're not going to leave me alone until I answer."

Jonah picked the phone up from the table and looked at the screen. "Looks like your friend found *Proteus*."

Adrenaline surged through her veins at the information. *Proteus* was one of the most dangerous men in the world. He was the mastermind of too many crimes to count, but there was never enough evidence to pursue. Only statements from witnesses that never managed to survive let them know that he existed at all.

Audrey caught the phone with one hand and glanced at the screen, feeling her blood chill at the information there. She looked up in time to watch Jonah pull the trigger.

The fact that the bullet was silenced didn't make it hurt any less when it pierced her chest. The force of it knocked her against the headboard and she struggled to breathe as what felt like molten lead burned through her lungs.

She stared at the face of her partner—her lover—and she knew she couldn't hide her surprise. She'd never suspected. Never thought he could be

Proteus. And now she'd be dead because of it.

"Surprised, love?"

She sucked in a breath and heard the whistling sound from her lungs. There was no use trying to speak.

"As you can understand, it's time for me to leave. You'll have to go through debriefing by yourself. Though I'm not sure they care much at the morgue."

His smile was a slash of cruelty and his eyes were cold as ice. Her lips were wet and she tasted the blood as it bubbled from her mouth.

"Thanks for giving me the name of your informant. I'll take care of him immediately. And thanks for the fuck. It was definitely—memorable."

Her gun was in the nightstand drawer. She might have a chance if she could just get to it in time, but she wasn't sure she could move her arm. She focused on breathing and put the pain away as she'd been trained to do. Her mind zeroed in on the area of her body where the bullet had pierced, slowing the beat of her heart so her blood didn't pump from the wound quite as fast. She knew how to survive. It was these skills Mossad excelled at over the American agencies.

Jonah began to dress quickly and he started scattering things across the room, tossing tables and their belongings about. But he kept his eye on her. He knew her training better than anyone. Knew that she could be just as deadly while wounded.

Audrey's time was running out and she'd never have a better opportunity to try and take him down. She made her move and pulled out the drawer, reaching for the gun inside, but the agony of another bullet had her slumping against the blood soaked mattress.

"You could never hope to be better than me, love. You're too soft. It's why you failed as a Mossad agent and why you've failed now. Didn't I tell you to never trust anyone? Even your partner? I told you we all have secrets."

She didn't even feel the third bullet as it entered her body. Her eyesight dimmed and the only sound was her waning heartbeat and the soft click of the door as he left her there to die.

CHAPTER ONE

Present Day

Hospitals reminded him of death—the cloying antiseptic that didn't quite mask the bitter smell of urine and blood, and the insistent beep of machines that pumped life into the fragile human body.

When it came his time to go, he'd rather be taken out swiftly—in the line of duty preferably—without having to linger and waste away while a machine allowed him a few more precious breaths.

Archer Ryan waited patiently as the elevator rose to the top floor, his hands relaxed by his sides, and none of the nerves he felt at being in a hospital visible. He understood why the meeting had to be here, but he didn't have to like it. Especially since he'd been called back early from vacation. The time spent with his daughter was precious, even more so since it was limited to holidays and summer vacations. But he'd come anyway.

The elevator dinged and the doors opened. The scents and sounds were different here than the rest of the hospital. This was the private wing, and most of the money to build it had been donated by the MacKenzie family. It looked more like a hotel than a hospital—the walls were painted a soft green and the rooms were suites, so the families of the sick could be comfortable while they waited to see if their loved ones would live or die.

The carpet, soft and plush beneath his feet, silenced his steps, and he handed his security identification to the nurse at the front desk so she could scribble his name.

It had been eight weeks since an explosion had almost ended Shane MacKenzie's life just outside the MacKenzie Security compound in Surrender, Montana. The damage to his body had been terrible to witness, but Shane's cousin Thomas had managed to keep him alive until a helicopter could airlift him to the hospital. There'd been no possible way to save the leg that had been lost in the explosion. It had been a miracle he hadn't lost them both.

For six of those eight weeks Shane had been in a coma, every day a new roll of the dice. The swelling around the brain had worried the doctors more than anything, and they'd warned Shane's family that his mind might never be the same.

Archer had known Shane a few years now, and he couldn't imagine what the former Navy SEAL Commander was going through. Shane was meant for active duty, and according to Shane's older brother Declan—and Archer's boss—Shane wasn't fighting very hard to live.

The MacKenzie family had been taking turns at the hospital, making sure there was always a familiar face for Shane to see. Declan had set up a makeshift office in the little lounge area attached to Shane's room, and more often than not, there were other MacKenzies in and out as well. The security company was a family business after all, and Declan was the heart of it. Anyone who knew anything about MacKenzies understood that they always stood together, through the good times and the bad. And this definitely constituted as bad.

Dec had called while Archer had been lounging on a beach in Hawaii with his daughter, Stella. She'd just turned sixteen and was growing up before his eyes, and he'd wanted to give them both a memorable vacation before she started back to school the following week. He wouldn't have too many more years to enjoy her all to himself. She'd grown into a beautiful young woman, but she lived with her mother—his ex-wife—in Northern California, and between his job and her school schedule, their time together was much too infrequent.

The door that led into Shane MacKenzie's suite of rooms was open, but Archer knocked before he stepped inside. Declan MacKenzie sat behind a desk that had been set up in front of the group of windows that looked out on the parking lot. He commanded it as if hospitals were his normal place of business—his laptop open and the sleeves of his shirt rolled to the elbows as he talked softly into his cell phone.

The MacKenzies were all cut from the same cloth. When you saw the five siblings together, there was no doubt they were related. They all had hair as black as pitch and an arresting combination of physical features that made you look twice in their direction. Dec's eyes were gray as fog and one didn't have to look at them long to know that he wasn't a man to be messed with. The scar that ran along his jawline only added to the sense of danger.

Declan nodded at Archer when he came in the room and pointed to one of the chairs in front of the desk. Dec looked like a man who'd had too little sleep and too much worry.

It had been Declan's fiancé, Sophia, who Shane had been protecting when the missile had exploded. She was safe now, and the man who'd tried to kill her was dead, but Shane's future was still very much in the air.

Dec hung up the phone and leaned back in his chair with a sigh, rubbing his hand over his face.

"Thanks for coming," he said. "I'm sorry to cut your vacation short."

Archer settled back in his own chair and crossed his ankle over his knee. "I figured if you were calling me back from vacation, then it was probably important."

"How's Stella?"

"Pissed you cut her Hawaiian vacation short." Archer grinned at Dec. "She says you can make it up to her later though. She suggested you give me a raise so I can buy her the car she's been begging for."

Declan snorted out a laugh. "Christ, I can't believe she's driving. Seems like yesterday she was asking for piggyback rides."

"That's what happens when you get old. Don't worry, it won't be too long before you have your own kids asking for piggyback rides."

The look on Declan's face was content, despite the stress of the last weeks. He'd finally ended up with the woman he'd loved for years, and Archer was happy for his friend. Declan wasn't just his boss. Archer had worked many a black ops mission with Declan before they'd both decided to get out of the game. It had been a no brainer to follow Declan when he'd opened his own security company.

"How's Shane?" Archer looked to the connecting doorway that led to Shane's hospital room. The beep of monitors was soft and he could hear the low hum of the television in the background.

Dec's face said it all—the worry and anguish were plain to see. "His body is healing. The doctor said the area where they amputated is healing well. They were able to save the knee, which will be helpful when he's ready to wear a prosthetic. His other leg has had two surgeries already and pins were put in, but everything is looking fine there. They don't think he'll have to have any more surgeries on that leg, just a couple of skin grafts. The ribs are still giving him a little trouble, but the doctor said that was to be expected since they were cracked. His last brain scan was clear."

"But?"

Dec blew out a long breath. "He still isn't speaking. To any of us. He's shut himself off, just staring at the T.V. or the wall. My mother is in there with him now. She reads to him and talks to him. We all do. But he never responds. He won't talk to the trauma psychologist that keeps coming by or the doctors who monitor his progress."

"It's understandable, Dec. He's had his whole world taken from him. Commanding that team was his life. And he'll never lead them again."

"I know. And he's so fucking angry I just keep waiting for him to blow. You can't see it by looking at him, but I know my brother. His eyes are dead. I've seen men who had eyes like that, and nothing good came from it. And that terrifies me. His rage is festering beneath the surface, and until he lets it loose he'll never start to heal. At least on an emotional level. I don't know what to do for him."

For the first time Archer could recall, Declan looked helpless, and he had no idea what to do for his friend to make it better.

"You know I'll do whatever I can to help."

Dec pulled a file from beneath the massive stack of papers on his desk and tossed it to Archer. "Yeah, well, that's why I called you back early. I need to stay close by for now and I think you and I are the only two people suited to this job."

Meaning that the job required black ops training. Archer raised an eyebrow at that. "I'm listening."

"What do you know about Oblivion?"

"Just whispers really. Only that it exists. It's an off the books spook organization. The areas they work are murky at best and always dangerous. Even my security clearance didn't allow for much more information than that."

Dec nodded as if that's what he expected. "Three years ago, team members of Oblivion were contracted to find and terminate *Proteus*."

Archer let out a low whistle between his teeth and felt his adrenaline surge. He and Dec had both had run-ins with the terrorist known as *Proteus* in the past. They'd never won against him.

"Oblivion was able to link *Proteus* to a man named Francois Renard. Renard was a broker, and the one *Proteus* most often used. Somehow *Proteus* found out about the link and had Renard taken and held in an abandoned military base in France."

"A leak on the inside?"

"Suspected, but never proven. Oblivion knew Renard had been taken and had a team sent out to observe and assess whether an extraction was possible. It turns out *Proteus* was always a step ahead of the ops team. He'd planned that the team would try to rescue Renard and booby-trapped the whole place with explosives.

"It was run as a standard op. The scouts went in first, taking out guards and clearing the areas. Two agents were assigned to go in specifically for Renard and bring him out. Agents Jonah Salt and Audrey Sharpe."

"Oh, damn." Archer felt his blood run cold. Bits and pieces of what had happened on that mission had trickled to different parts of the agency. It was impossible to keep everything quiet. But they'd done a pretty good job of it. Whatever happened in France had been sealed and buried deep in the CIA vaults.

"Making a long story short, the base was blown to shit and so were most of the agents inside. A couple made it out with critical wounds. Salt and Sharpe had barely reached the perimeter when the blast went off, no doubt a timing miscalculation on

Proteus's part or we'd have found their body parts along with the other agents. They made it out and managed to get back to their safe point to wait for extraction."

"I remember hearing about parts of this before they swept it under the rug." You couldn't belong to the agency without knowing who Jonah Salt was.

"Yeah. The two of them missed their meet for extraction, so undercover agents were dispatched to check out the scene and see what had gone wrong. They found Sharpe's body. She'd been shot three times in the chest and was hanging on by a thread when the team got there. The room had been ransacked and Salt was nowhere to be found. Sharpe died twice on the table during surgery."

"But she's alive?"

"She's alive. They never found Salt's body. His car went over the side of a cliff and there wasn't anything left to find. They pulled parts of the wreckage up, but there wasn't enough conclusive evidence to show tampering. There was, however, evidence of another car being involved, an extra pair of skid marks along with Salt's that went to the edge of the cliff. Someone knew who they were and hired a hit on both of them."

"Please tell me you didn't call me in to search

for *Proteus*. I'm good, boss, but I think that's a job for more than one man."

"Hell, I'd trust you to take *Proteus* out before any of those new recruits they've replaced us with. Jesus, they're infants."

Archer grinned. It felt like they'd barely been older than that when they started.

"But no. That's not your assignment. I want you to bring in Audrey Sharpe."

Archer raised a brow in confusion. "Bring her in for what? Isn't she the agency's problem?"

"She resigned her position with the agency while she was still in the hospital recovering. And then as soon as she was able, she disappeared. Oblivion has been looking for her, but not with much enthusiasm. They never got to fully debrief her. They figured she was PTSD and it was best to let her go."

"What do you think?"

"I think she's as capable as ever. Her background is impressive. She was Mossad before she was recruited by the agency. *Kidon*."

"Jesus. And they just let her go?"

"She'd been shot three times and left for dead. And that's after she'd already survived being tortured by the Syrians some years before. They thought she'd be ineffective."

"But you don't."

"No. I want her for MacKenzie Security. We need another agent and she's more than qualified. And Oblivion might not be worried about what she knows, but she knows something. I've been following her pattern. She's hunting. Trying to stay off the grid as much as possible."

Declan smiled when he said it and Archer let out a short laugh. Dec could find anyone, anywhere. It didn't matter how off the grid they were.

"All of the information is in the file. You'll pick up her trail. Convince her to come back with you."

"And what about this personal mission she seems to be on?"

"Help her if need be. Or see if she'll abandon it altogether. We need her, and the sooner the better. I'm taking myself out of the field. The idea of being away from Sophia and a warm bed isn't all that appealing. And the business has reached the point where I do more good behind a desk than in front of it."

Archer ignored the pang of envy he felt whenever he looked at Declan. They'd shared similar lives and worked for the same organizations, but Archer didn't feel the same contentment that his friend did. His marriage had failed—because his wife couldn't handle not knowing about the secret missions and whether he'd come back alive—and he'd been young and arrogant enough to not bother trying to convince her that what they had was worth fighting and working for.

Now his daughter was being raised by another man. Granted, his ex-wife's husband seemed like a good guy and he was good to Stella, but Archer was jealous that the other man was the one getting to see his daughter grow into a woman.

But he'd blown his chance. Which was why Declan was sending him on this mission and not one of the other agents who had a family. He'd bring Audrey Sharpe back with him and then he'd go on the next mission, and then the next after that. And he wouldn't think about being content. He'd think about surviving.

"I'll bring her in for you," Archer finally said, grabbing the file and opening it. And then he felt the air whoosh out of his lungs and his heart pump faster. The photograph was taken from her CIA file, but there was nothing ordinary about the woman in it. Her face was clear of cosmetics or any enhancements, and still he had trouble believing what he was seeing.

Audrey Sharpe was the most breathtaking woman he'd ever laid eyes on. In the photo, dark hair was pulled back from an oval face. Her cheekbones were high, her chin slightly pointed, and her nose small and straight. Dark brows winged over almond shaped eyes the color of melted chocolate, and he felt his body stir as he scrutinized the photo and looked for flaws. There weren't any that he could see. Her lips were full and ripe and he wondered what they'd feel like against his skin. His cock spiked to full attention and his balls drew tight against his body, and he repositioned the file in his lap so he was covered.

"You've got to be fucking kidding me," he said, looking at Declan's amused grin. "No fucking way was this woman Mossad or a member of Oblivion. She'd stick out like a sore thumb."

"Don't be deceived by her looks. Mossad has a long history of recruiting beautiful and deadly women for just that purpose. I'd pit her skills against yours and mine any day."

"I have a feeling I'm going to hate this

assignment." He'd never reacted to a woman, much less a photograph, like he had when looking at Audrey Sharpe. He couldn't imagine what the impact would be when he saw her up close and in person.

Archer turned the photo facedown, hoping to get the image of her out of his head, but there was another behind it. It took several seconds for him to comprehend what he was seeing.

"Jesus Christ." Where her face was a study in sheer beauty, her back was gruesome in its display of cruelty. Thick white scars marred almost every inch of skin where she'd obviously been flogged. Scars on top of scars. And along her ribs the skin was puckered where it had been burned.

"From her time with the Syrians," Declan explained. "She didn't talk, so the torture went on for almost seventy-two hours before U.S. agents were able to extract her."

Cold fury slid through Archer at the thought of what she'd endured. But he turned to the next photograph, wanting—no needing—to see it all. The next photograph showed the front of her torso. The burn scars extended to the front of her ribs and just beneath her breasts, though her breasts remained untouched and smooth, making the scars seem all the more monstrous.

This photograph must have been the most recent, because three white bandages were placed over the wounds from where she'd been shot. It was a miracle the one in her upper chest hadn't pierced her heart.

Archer nodded and looked at Declan. "This much injury can damage the mind as well as the body."

Declan looked beyond him to the room where his brother lay. "Sometimes it can. But there are special people in the world that are worth pulling out of the abyss. I believe she'll be worth it."

"She's not going to want to come with me. If you say she's hunting, then she's got an agenda and nothing will make her stray from that."

Dec's lips twitched. "I guess that means you'll be helping her. Call me if there's trouble and I'll spare a couple of extra men, but I think she'll be more agreeable if it's just you. We wouldn't want to scare her off."

"A woman who's been tortured and left for dead isn't likely to scare easily."

Dec smiled again and the scar along his jaw tightened. "Just make sure you're not the one with your tail tucked between your legs at the end of it. MacKenzie Security has a reputation to uphold."

Archer shot Dec the finger, making him laugh. "It takes more than one woman to have me running scared."

Declan waited until Archer was out the door before murmuring, "We'll see, my friend. We'll see."

***

Shane MacKenzie listened to the conversation his brother was having in the next room. Declan was wrong. There wasn't rage inside of him. There was nothing—an emptiness that was so vast he couldn't believe it didn't reach up and swallow him whole.

You had to be alive to feel anger. And as far as he was concerned, he wasn't alive. His life had been the SEAL team he'd commanded. The men who'd become as close as his brothers. The men he'd have died for. What good was he now? Half a man and useless at that. And now his team had a new commander and they were back out of the country on a mission Shane would never know about. He'd been discharged. Honorably and with valor. But what fucking good did medals do when all he wanted was to get up and walk again—to lead again?

Weakness invaded his body. He could barely move. Couldn't even take a piss without someone there to help him. His mother sat in the corner, glancing at him occasionally with worry and helplessness on her face. He'd heard her crying when she'd thought he was asleep.

He turned his head so he wouldn't have to look at her and stared at the opposite wall. The machines continued to beep, but he noticed the one that monitored his pulse was moving faster than normal. Maybe he was a little angry after all.

CHAPTER TWO

For three years, her sole purpose in life had been to track down *Proteus*. And kill him.

She made no excuses for what she'd decided to do. She only knew the man known as *Proteus* had to be stopped. It was easier to think of him as *Proteus* and not Jonah Salt—former mentor and lover. And she'd be lying if she didn't admit that revenge at what he'd done to her didn't weigh in on her decision to take him out. But it was only part of the reason.

He'd put three bullets in her chest, leaving her for dead after she'd given him her trust—something she'd never given lightly and would never give again. To anyone. Then he'd left her for dead and gone for her friend Shai, who'd given her *Proteus's* identity in the first place. Shai's body had been found in the Jordan River with his throat slit along with evidence of prolonged torture—his back teeth had been missing as well as his genitalia.

Salt had always been a good interrogator, and she had no doubt that by the time he was finished, Shai had given him names of anyone else who knew *Proteus's* identity, as well as where he kept his computers where the information was stored.

Yes, she wanted revenge. But that was just a side benefit. Salt was a threat to all humankind. And the lives he'd taken, and would continue to take, were why she needed to end him.

No one else had been as close to him as she had. He'd helped train her and had been her partner. Who else would know how to hunt him better than she did?

She'd slipped out from under the agency and gone her own way. And it hadn't been easy, because Jonah was very good at what he did. She liked to think she was better. Like any agent, she had safe houses scattered in different countries that held bags of cash, new identities and weapons. They'd allowed her to survive and blend during her time off the grid.

It had taken her months to recover from the

gunshot wounds enough to go out on her own. They told her she'd died twice on the operating table and was lucky to be alive. She believed in a higher power and understood that she'd been spared so she could finish this last task. Part of her knew she wouldn't come back from this mission alive. And she'd made peace with that.

After leaving the hospital, it had taken another six months to get herself back into shape so she could fight without getting her ass handed to her on a plate. Her body was stronger now than it had even been before her accident, her muscles honed and lean. The scars from the bullets were only another reminder of her mistakes. Mistakes she'd never make again.

It had taken her another six months to get a trace of Jonah's whereabouts. He'd laid low for a while, avoiding most of the terrorist activities *Proteus* had been suspected of. Jonah was arrogant, and that was going to be his downfall. Her patience finally paid off when she'd picked up his trail along the Kamchatka and Russian border.

She had a safe house up in the mountains. It was time to regroup and restock her weapons since she'd had to leave her others behind before crossing the border. She only had the knife in her boot and her fists for protection. It was enough. But one could never be too prepared.

It hadn't been hard to pass through unnoticed. She spoke the language like a native. And no one paid any attention as she started the climb up the mountains to where her safe house was located. She'd only been there once before. Had only needed it once before. But her memory had never failed her.

The weather was brisk and wind slapped at her face the higher into the mountains she climbed. Her jacket was made out of a special material that was thin enough to give her freedom of movement if she needed it, but was as warm as any heavy coat. Neoprene gloves covered her hands for the same reason. They weren't the warmest, but they wouldn't impede her if she needed to fight.

The higher she climbed the more quiet it became, and the little hairs on the back of her neck began to stand on end. The temperature had dropped a good thirty degrees and snow crunched beneath her boots as she continued to climb.

There were little signs that most people wouldn't pay attention to—broken twigs or the displacement of small rocks. But she wasn't most people. The mountain was silent, no birds or wildlife to be heard, and because it was silent she walked an extra mile around the perimeter where her cabin was located. She pulled the knife from her boot and waited—just listening—ignoring the white puffs of air that escaped her mouth and the way the cold made her muscles twinge where she'd been wounded.

She crept closer and closer until the cabin was in sight, but she knew by looking at it that Jonah was already gone. He'd definitely been there, though. And he'd left a gift for her to find.

Audrey secured the house first, making sure he wasn't waiting to ambush her, before she came back around to the front. The body was placed just in front of the steps to the front door, so you'd have to step over him to get in.

She didn't recognize him, only that he'd been a man of some importance. He was dressed in full military regalia and had enough badges and medals pinned to his chest for her to know he'd been in command.

Jonah never did anything without a reason, and leaving the body here was significant, though she wasn't sure why. He'd laid the body out like it would be inside of a casket, with arms crossed over the chest and the ankles crossed as well. His throat had been slit, and the blood had turned the snow beneath him brown. The man's eyes were closed, which meant Jonah had made them that way, and a light dusting of snow covered his eyelashes and hair.

The weather made time of death tricky to pinpoint, but she was guessing the kill was right around twenty-four hours old. Audrey had wondered if Jonah would feel her closing in on him. It didn't worry her, but it did complicate matters. Now it would become a game, to see who could outmaneuver the other.

The Russian military would miss this man, whoever he was, which meant she needed to get what she could and get out as fast as possible before she had the Russians on her trail. She didn't have time for another complication.

She left the body where it lay and approached the cabin, stopping in front of the door. The number *165* was written on the lintel, and when she touched her fingers to it, she realized Jonah had used the blood from the man at her feet to write it.

Definitely a game. He was emulating The Passover with the blood over the doorframe because of her Jewish faith, letting her know that this message was meant for her and no other.

Audrey reached down and gathered a handful of snow and then rubbed it across the numbers, wiping them away until the snow in her hand melted red. The number would be committed to her memory forever and there was no reason to give whoever would come after her any clues.

The cabin could be wired for explosives. It was a trap she'd considered and discarded. Jonah would want to see this played out and he'd wait before he tried to kill her again. So she was safe. Probably.

She tested the doorknob and found it unlocked, and then she pushed the door wide and stepped inside. It looked exactly as it had the last time she'd seen it. She'd been Mossad then, but a safe house was a safe house. All agents had them, no matter what country they served, and she'd thought this one would be safe from Jonah. She had no idea how he'd found out about it.

The floors were wood and barren, with nothing scattered about to get in the way of an easy exit. A single twin bed was shoved in the corner with blankets folded on top of it. There was canned food in the cupboards and a wood burning stove.

Audrey went to the bed and shoved it across the floor so it screeched against the wood, and she knew by looking at the boards beneath that Jonah had found her stash. But she pried up the loose board anyway and stared down into the empty space.

"Fuck."

She grabbed a penlight from her belt and knelt down, shining the light and running her hands along the sides of the small crawlspace. She was looking for the next part of his message. Obviously the number *165* was a coordinate, and considering where they were the distance wouldn't be too far. Etched in the dirt in the far corner was the number *66*.

"Not too far away at all." She plugged the numbers she had into her handheld device so it could start searching for possible routes and locations by process of elimination. She stood and dusted off her hands. He'd taken her extra clothes and the main stash of weapons and supplies she'd kept inside.

"Asshole."

The cabin groaned and creaked from the cold, settling into itself as she took stock. Annoyance and frustration bit at her and her first thought was to rush through and see if he'd found her reserve stocks, but she held herself back and centered her focus on the room itself. He wanted her to find him, for whatever reason, but he wasn't going to make it easy on her.

"There you are, you bastard." One of the cupboard doors was ever so slightly ajar. It wasn't noticeable unless you compared it to the order of the rest of the room.

On her way to the cupboard she stopped at the little stone fireplace and stuck her hand up inside it. Her fingers brushed against the gun taped inside the chimney and she ripped it down, at once feeling more at ease with it in her possession.

She held the gun down at her side and approached the cupboard door, edging it the rest of the way open with her finger. And there it was, written in pencil this time. *0800*. And just beneath that was a *51W*.

Audrey looked at the watch on her wrist and swore. Wherever she was going she had less than twelve hours to get there. She needed the other coordinate and she needed it fast.

But there was no coordinate to be found. At least not on the inside of the house. She put her gun at the small of her back and stepped back over the body of the man at the base of the outside stairs. Sunset was still a couple of hours off, but she needed to be gone before dark fell and the chances of an ambush rose. She'd prefer not to traverse unfamiliar Russian soil in the middle of the night.

Hers were the only footprints visible in the area. Snow would have fallen between the time Jonah left and when she arrived, making her assumption right that it had been at least twenty-four hours since he'd been there, as snow tended to fall nightly and disappear in the daytime during that time of year.

She made her way to the back of the cabin and the small woodpile stacked waist high. A light sheen of sweat covered her skin as she moved all the wood, exposing the secondary trap door she'd built into the ground. She brushed off dead grass and dirt to reveal the rusted iron strongbox she'd buried.

The lid protested as she pulled at it, and eventually gave way with a sound similar to nails on a chalkboard. A sigh of relief she hadn't realized she'd been holding in escaped when she saw the items inside it had been untouched. A secondary cache of money, a new I.D., extra hunting knives, a .9mm pistol with an extra magazine, and a long-range rifle.

She worked quickly, outfitting herself for easy access to her weapons, and then assembled the rifle and strapped it to her back. The sun was barely visible above the trees and she still hadn't found the last coordinate marker.

With fierce determination, Audrey searched the cabin looking for the last number. She stopped in front of the body Jonah had laid out so precisely and tried to get into the mind of a brilliant criminal.

The position of the body was purposeful. Jonah had laid the man out for burial. The head was facing east, an important detail in many religious ceremonies. She was missing something important.

She knelt by the man and said a small prayer, wishing his soul safe travels into the afterlife, and then she went about the task of searching his body. His hands were empty and there were no marks on his skin discernable to the naked eye. And then her eye caught the glint of metal on his chest, reflected in the last rays of the sun.

"13th Infantry. 13 North. That should do it."

Now she just had to figure out how to navigate her way across the Bering Strait and make sure she did the last thing Jonah Salt would ever expect.

CHAPTER THREE

It turned out the last thing Jonah would expect her to do was to come in by water.

The coordinates he'd left her led her back into U.S. territory, north of Nome, Alaska. The exact location was in the middle of the water, and there was nothing nearby except oil rigs, tankers, and a smattering of whaling and fishing vessels.

The time frame Jonah had given her had been just enough for her to find a plane and fly herself back into the States. There was one advantage to such an isolated area; it was easy to enter and leave without notice. She landed the seaplane she'd "borrowed" some ways out from shore and used the inflatable life raft in the back of the plane to paddle to shore.

SIZZLE

Salt would expect her to come for him by land, to set up a trap and take him out as he made his way back onto soil. She'd never be as good as him on the water. It was just fact, and he knew it. Jonah had gone through BUD/S training with the SEALs, and was mentally and physically at home at sea. He'd never expect her to come at him from the water. Audrey would only have one shot to catch him by surprise.

Stars glittered unusually bright in this part of the world. By Alaska standards, Nome was a large town, but it still had a population of less than four thousand people. She looked through her night vision goggles, getting the layout of the land. The town itself was nestled on a small flat area of land, but the surrounding areas were hilly and the terrain difficult. A thick covering of snow blanketed everything and it smelled as if more could be coming. She'd be able to assess better in the daylight.

Fishing and whaling boats were scattered haphazardly—different makes, models and sizes—and hooked to rough hewn docks along the shoreline. They floated lazily in ice-crusted waters, well used and rusted with age. There wasn't much movement in the town, but the docks were already busy with those getting ready to take their boats out.

Audrey paid a fisherman named Jerry—who in her opinion needed to head back home and sleep it off—handsomely for the use of his boat. It was smaller than the others along the shoreline, more maneuverable, and the engine sounded smooth and fast when he started it up. Jerry might be a drunk, but he took good care of his equipment.

She set out on the cold and choppy waters, the sea black as pitch and the stars and a sliver of moon the only light in the sky. Droplets of icy water splashed on her face and clothes and her breath clouded white with every breath she took. The wind cut like a scalpel and made her joints stiff if she stood still too long.

The coordinates Jonah had given her were programmed into her watch, and she turned the engine of the boat off when it buzzed on her wrist, telling her she'd arrived at her destination. She still had half an hour to prep and get set up. Now she only had to wait and watch, and hope she hadn't miscalculated Jonah's expectations of her.

The darkness was both her friend and her enemy. She'd be concealed for a time, giving her the edge she needed. But it would make the shot she'd have to take even more difficult, despite the infrared scope on her rifle.

The long shots weren't her specialty. She could

make them, but to be accurate she needed time and intense concentration. Almost perfect conditions. The choppy water and harsh winds were going to be a factor, and she had to make the shot count.

She set up her rifle and scanned the waters through her scope, flexing her fingers to keep them loose. A tanker almost completely concealed the Zodiac anchored next to it. She would've missed it completely if she'd been set up to take the shot on land. That's what he'd been hoping for. He wanted to draw her out. There wasn't a good place for cover on land. There were no trees to speak of and hiding in the hills would've made the distance too great to make an accurate shot.

It was obvious he'd come early to do whatever task he'd assigned himself—nothing good if his past was anything to go by. But Jonah had planned to be finished by the time he'd given her and then he'd expect her to fall into whatever trap he'd set for her. Because he thought he knew her, understood her. When what he'd really done was underestimate the strength of her anger.

The water rippled just before he broke the surface next to the Zodiac and she watched as he rolled in with the experience of hundreds of missions at sea. He spit the rebreather out of his mouth and tossed it in the bottom of the boat. The water and winds were cold, so he kept the neoprene mask pulled down over his face.

She didn't need to see his face. She recognized the way he moved—the relaxed movements that spoke of someone completely at ease in the water. She recognized the breadth of his shoulders and the cruel slash of his smile as he checked the time at his wrist. He was waiting for her, and as if he'd read her mind he picked up his infrared binoculars and looked toward the shore.

He lay flat in the Zodiac and it was then he picked up the rifle that had been laying at the bottom and tried to set his sights on her.

"You son of a bitch." As if her words had carried the distance across the water he turned and his gaze met hers through the binoculars. She took the shot before he could roll himself back into the water.

She'd aimed for the center of his chest, the largest target she had, but her aim and his movement had altered the course of the bullet and she'd seen it enter his shoulder instead.

"Dammit." Her only hope was that the bullet had hit something vital. She crawled her way back to the engine and started the boat up, not caring that Jonah could see her now. Gunfire sounded and she heard the ping as a bullet glanced off the side of the boat. She'd gotten him in the right shoulder, so he'd be shooting left handed. He wasn't as proficient using the other hand, but he was still pretty damned accurate.

Her only goal was to get back to land. He'd have to spare precious seconds to stop and bind the wound so he didn't lose too much blood, and those seconds were what she needed to make her escape.

At this time of the year, dawn came late and was just rising over the horizon by the time she docked. Sunlight glared in her eyes and off the water, and she wasn't sure she'd ever seen a sunrise quite so bright.

Her adrenaline surged as she hopped down to the rickety dock and used the boat for cover, knowing it wasn't out of the realm of possibility for Jonah to be closer on her trail than she estimated. She still wasn't out of the woods and wouldn't be. Not until Jonah Salt was dead.

Jerry sat in his lawn chair on the snow covered dock with a blanket spread over his lap and the smell of hundred proof something reeking out the top of his flask. He eyed the boat and then his gaze went to her and he wheezed out a gin soaked breath as she passed him another wad of bills as a thank you. She didn't realize until it was too late what had seemed off about Jerry. He'd had guilty eyes.

She felt the air move behind her just before a black sack was tossed over her head. She kicked out blindly, but against so many she knew she was better off saving her energy. Her hands and feet were bound and she was tossed unceremoniously into the backseat of a car. A foot shoved her to the floorboard and then gave her another small kick as someone got into the backseat with her. She heard the distinct sound of a bullet being chambered into a gun and went completely still.

But it was the rapid spatter of Russian that had her breathing out a sigh of relief. It wasn't Jonah who'd found her. At least not yet.

CHAPTER FOUR

It had been three weeks since Declan had passed on the assignment to bring in Audrey Sharpe. Archer had to hand it to Dec, he never hired anyone who wasn't the best of the best. And Audrey Sharpe was pretty damned good.

If he hadn't read her file from cover to cover, memorizing her patterns and trying to get inside her head and see how her mind worked, then he probably never would have found her. And he hated to admit it, but luck had been as much of a factor as his skill with this job. If he hadn't seen her get tossed into the back seat of an SUV, she more than likely would've been long gone by the time he got close enough to make contact.

She'd been alive when they'd bound her hands

and tossed the black cloth bag over her head, so he wasn't particularly worried about her safety for the time being. He was more curious as to why Russian intelligence agents wanted her. It had been a while since he'd used the language, but from his hiding place, and the direction the wind was blowing, he heard and understood enough that they needed Audrey. At least for the time being.

Archer waited until the three all-terrain SUVs, one of which had Audrey in the backseat, started the drive north. There was only one road in that direction—a two-way stretch most people only used when they were headed to fish in the many rivers around the area. There were some abandoned campgrounds and the remains of a town that had once been popular during the gold rush, but the population had dwindled and the buildings had mostly fallen into disrepair. Only a couple of hundred people called it home now.

Archer waited a couple of minutes and then started up his Jeep to follow behind, turning the heat to high. He hit speed dial on his phone and then set the call to speaker so he could keep his hands free.

"MacKenzie," Declan barked out. "Someone had better be dead."

Archer's brows rose at the uncharacteristic display of irritation from his friend. Dec was about the most level-headed person he'd ever known, and he'd always said temper was counterproductive to getting the job done.

"Is this a bad time?" Archer asked.

On the other end of the line, Declan tried to get his brain in working order while Sophia wreaked havoc with his libido. They were having a lazy Saturday morning in bed, but no matter how much she was tempting him with that sweet mouth, he was the boss and he was always available to his agents.

"We're good, but make it fast." He narrowed his gaze and shook his head in warning at Sophia. And then his fingers dug into the sheets as she gave him a wicked smile and tucked the head of his cock between her plump lips.

"Jesus."

"Boss? You there?"

"Have you found Audrey Sharpe?" Dec tried thinking of anything and everything but Sophia's magic tongue and the way her hand tightened around the base of his cock and squeezed. She licked over the engorged head, sending electric impulses through his entire body.

His fingers threaded through her hair, and he

had the brief thought that he should hold her off, but instead he guided her down so she took him in completely, surrounding his cock with the wet warmth of her mouth. She was playing with fire, and he couldn't wait to return the favor.

"You could say that," Archer said. "I just watched a group of Russians toss her into the back of a car and drive away."

"What? Wait—" he said to Sophia and then sat up straighter in bed.

"Wait for what?" Archer asked, the confusion evident in his voice.

"Sorry, wasn't talking to you. Where are you? Is she still alive?"

"We're in Alaska. And she's alive. I'm following behind as we speak."

"It wouldn't be good for MacKenzie Security to have any disagreements with Russia. We've got several contracts for services at the moment."

"So noted. I'll make sure I'm not wearing my MacKenzie Security T-shirt when I kick their asses."

Dec's lips twitched and he relaxed against the headboard. Archer would take care of any situations and he'd protect MacKenzie Security. He could always count on Archer. Sophia made a satisfied hum in the back of her throat and continued her task of driving him crazy. His balls drew up tight against his body and he could feel the come building, waiting for release.

And then Sophia did the unthinkable and crawled up his body until she straddled his hips. His heart thudded in his chest and he leaned forward to nip at the plump breast she offered him. And then he held back a groan as she sank down on his cock with no mercy, her pussy clamping around him like a vise.

She couldn't hold back her own moan as she took him to the hilt, and he forgot about the agent waiting for some kind of response on the other end of the line. His fingers gripped the phone with one hand and Sophia's hip with the other. And then she threw her head back and began to ride and he was lost.

"Good work," Dec said, his voice strained as he reversed their positions so Sophia was flat on her back. He slid deep inside of her and watched her face as she climaxed beneath him. "Gotta go."

Archer's brow crooked at the sound of moans of pleasure being cut off as the phone disconnected.

Now he felt a little bit like a voyeur. And he was a little turned on, which made the situation even worse.

He blew out a breath and tried to remember the last time he'd had a woman in his bed. It had been too long to remember.

"Declan gets sex, and I'm chasing down Russians and a woman who doesn't want to be found. Life is so unfair."

***

Audrey probably would've disagreed with Archer's statement had she heard it. She very much wanted to be found.

After an hour-long car ride over a road that felt like it had been made completely of potholes, her legs and hands had fallen asleep. Fighting back would've been a useless effort when they stopped the car and pulled her out by the collar of her shirt. She immediately dropped to her knees since her legs wouldn't support her, and laughter erupted from those who circled her. Snow seeped through her black cargo pants and she was grateful for the neoprene skin suit she wore beneath them.

"Pick her up and bring her inside," one of the men said in Russian. "Stop playing."

Audrey's head hung down and the blood was rushing back to her extremities. Her skin prickled like it was being stuck with hot needles. She bit back a groan as they jerked her to her feet and pushed her forward. She'd managed to work her gloves off and she'd started loosening the ropes before she'd lost feeling in her hands, but she hadn't progressed far.

The black bag still covered her head, but she could see pinpricks of sunlight through the fabric. The smell of salt and sea was still strong, though the wind wasn't near as piercing as it had been closer to the shoreline.

Her feet kicked chunks of ice and snow as they led her about fifty yards from the car. The sunlight disappeared, shaded by the building they'd led her to, and she listened as a bolt cutter was used to cut through the lock.

"Hurry. Gregor wants us finished within the hour."

A laugh slithered against her skin and an arm curled around her body as a hand roughly squeezed her breast.

"Have you gotten a look at her face?" the man holding her said. "I'm not going to be done in an hour."

The other men laughed and Audrey had to resist the urge to fight against them. It was best to make them think she was weak so she had the advantage of surprise later.

The door slid open noisily, on rails that were in desperate need of oiling, and she felt the rush of air across her skin as it whooshed past. The smell of rotten fish over an underlying odor of motor oil and decaying meat had the gorge rising in the back of her throat, and she had to take a moment to breathe in shallow pants through her mouth.

"Go," he said, shoving her through the opening. The door slid closed behind her with an ominous clank that sent sweat snaking down her spine.

Footsteps crunched over the broken concrete floor and they pushed her further inside—another thirty steps. They untied her hands and she flexed them to get the blood flowing again and then hands unzipped her jacket and stripped it down her arms. She was left in the long sleeved black thermal top, but without the jacket there was a noticeable difference in the temperature.

Multiple hands patted her down, taking the weapon at the small of her back, the knife sheathed at her wrist, and the other knife in her boot. They turned her around and shoved her again so the backs of her legs hit something hard, and at the same time hands pushed down on her shoulders so she was sitting in a chair.

Her arms were jerked back, straining the muscles in her shoulders, and they retied her hands. Whoever was tying them wasn't as experienced as the last person because she was able to get her hands in a position where there'd be extra room to maneuver. They bound each of her ankles to a chair leg, and then the bag was jerked off her head.

Audrey blinked a couple of times as her eyesight adjusted, and then felt a sharp sting against her face as one of the men backhanded her, snapping her head back. She tasted blood from where her teeth had cut the inside of her cheek and she spat it out at his feet.

"Bitch," he said in perfect English.

And then she smiled and relaxed back against the chair. The ropes that banded her wrists together burned as she worked at them.

She took note of her surroundings, calculating the best route of escape. The warehouse was large, obviously abandoned, and the only light coming in was from the sun shining through broken out windows and leaving grotesque shadows on the floors.

Old boat parts littered the space and it didn't take her long to find the cause of the awful smell. Whale carcasses were in different stages of decomposition along the side of the warehouse. Natives were allowed to legally hunt and kill a certain number of whales per year for the meat and oil, but the practice was illegal to anyone else. It looked like someone was using the warehouse to hide the contraband.

Windows were spaced evenly on one side, and even though most of the glass was broken out, they were covered by chicken wire and wouldn't be a viable means of escape. There was only one door in and out that she could see. Things were not looking good.

"You've gotten in our way, Ms. Sharpe," said a man from the back of the pack. She recognized his voice as the one who'd told the others to stop playing with her. The others moved to either side of her, leaving a direct line of sight between her and the man in charge.

Audrey continued to stare at him but didn't say anything. She was as curious for information as they were. He was older than the others and clearly the leader. The scruff on his face was silver, and a black watch cap was pulled low over his head. He'd stripped off his jacket and gloves so he only wore a black T-shirt and cargo pants, which was never a good sign. It meant things were probably going to get messy.

"I've studied you. I know of your past with the man Jonah Salt and that you are hunting him now. Why?"

She continued to stare at him and he smiled before wrapping her hair around his fist and yanking her head back. A knife pricked at her throat and she smelled the coppery tang of blood as the blade bit into her skin.

"I could slit your throat," he whispered, his face so close his whiskers scratched her cheek.

"It would be hard for me to talk if you did," she answered in Russian, turning her head slightly to meet his gaze.

He nodded in what she thought might be approval and moved the knife away slowly. "Yes, well, maybe we should start with other parts of the body. But I've been known to play nice. For instance, my name is Alexsei." He let go of her hair and backed away a step, but he didn't put the knife away. "It is good for a captive to know her captor, wouldn't you agree?"

"It certainly makes it more convenient to track

you down later," she said dryly.

He ignored her attempt at humor and began cleaning his fingernails with the tip of his knife. "We've been looking for Jonah Salt for a while now. It was only by chance that we stumbled across you trying to do the same."

Audrey arched a brow. What in the hell would the Russians want with Jonah? If she voiced the question, she'd owe them an answer. And they'd still probably try to kill her.

"If you're hunting him as well, what does it matter who catches him as long as he's dead?"

"That's the problem. We're not trying to kill him. Jonah Salt's death would be catastrophic for everyone."

"Maybe we're talking about a different Jonah Salt, because from where I'm standing his death could only be good."

The man smiled again and something about it had her blood chilling and her fingers working quicker at the ropes tying her hands.

"I'm telling you now to stop your hunt or you will die here today."

She saw the lie in his eyes. They planned for

her to die no matter what she agreed to. It was time to test them, to see what they really wanted with Jonah.

"I guess it's too bad I got a shot off just before you and your goons decided to kidnap me."

"You lie," he spat. Anger and something close to terror crossed his face.

"I'm not. He knew I was tracking him and miscalculated. He was expecting me to come at him from the opposite direction. He knows it'd be risky for me to take a shot from the water. Which is exactly what I did. And I succeeded." The confident smile she gave him did nothing to relieve the tension gathering inside her. Something was very wrong.

"Let me tell you what you've done, *piz'da*. Jonah Salt is the Russian Federation's number one enemy."

The fact that he'd just called her a cunt barely registered, because she was too surprised by the information he'd just imparted. If Salt was Russia's number one enemy, then they were keeping that information to themselves and not reaching out to other agencies to aid in his capture. That was never a good sign.

"As you know, our country relies on the sale of oil, particularly to the United States. Our economy would be devastated without that relationship. And Salt knows this. For the last year he has been holding a few of our tankers hostage. We have many, but he chooses only a handful, arming them with explosives. We do not know which tankers are armed. We only have the demonstration he sent us at the beginning."

Audrey's brow furrowed as she tried to recall details of what he might be talking about. And then she remembered. "The Krieg explosion," she said. "An oil tanker off the Pacific waters. The media called it a mini-Exxon Valdez, though the results weren't nearly as widespread. You're saying Salt was responsible?"

"He was. And he's rigged five other vessels. We don't know which ones or even where to begin searching. We only know that as long as we pay Salt his blackmail request of a million dollars per month, then he will not detonate the devices and bring an entire country to ruin."

"Smart of him," she said, thinking the entire scheme sounded like Jonah. "A steady stream of income. Not enough to draw attention to himself and not enough to break Russia's pocketbook. Very smart."

And horrific. She didn't need Alexsei to explain the ramifications of what would happen if those tankers blew. It'd be a worldwide disaster. Not only the environmental aspects—the affect it would have on water supplies, animals, sea life, and people. But it would also lead to the collapse of Russia's largest resource. An oil spill of that size in five difference locations would destroy them.

"So tell me, *sooka*. Did you leave him alive, or did you see him dead?"

"I'm getting tired of the name calling, Alexsei. And here I thought we were friends." Audrey thought quickly. Time was of the essence and there was no reason for her to hold information back from the Russians. It wasn't just their world that was in danger.

"You try my patience," he said, turning the knife in his hand. "I can either call you names or start cutting on your very delectable body."

"Fair enough," she said. "It was a shoulder shot, and it looked clean as far as I could tell. I'm not saying he couldn't succumb to blood loss or infection, but it wasn't a kill shot."

Alexsei nodded and gestured for two of his men to leave, presumably to start the search for a wounded Salt and save his worthless life. What hadn't come out in this conversation was the name of *Proteus*. She was starting to think that bit of information was her secret to keep. It was a bitter pill to swallow, knowing she'd have to save a man she'd wanted nothing more than to see dead.

Alexsei looked at her one last time and then to the men who still flanked her. "Kill her. And be quick about it."

Two men approached her from each side, one of them pulling his knife from the sheath at his waist just as the rope gave way on her wrists. She grabbed them by the shirtfronts and knocked their heads together, catching them both off guard with her freedom.

The knife slipped from one of the men's hands and she caught it, leaning down and cutting the rope wrapped around one of her ankles in one smooth motion. By this time, the other men standing around had recovered their surprise and were circling in. She didn't waste time and threw the knife at Alexsei, hitting him in the throat, and taking out the biggest threat first. The others she could deal with.

Audrey used one of the fallen men as leverage and swung her leg out, the chair still tied to one ankle so it swung in a wide arc, slamming it against two more men with a satisfying crunch against their heads.

SIZZLE

The last man came in low and fast and caught her around the middle, but the balance of the chair tied to her leg threw them both off and gave her time for her fingers to find the pressure points in his neck and render him unconscious.

His body collapsed on top of hers, releasing the air in her lungs in a great *whoosh* so she had to fight to suck in another breath. Her ankle was throbbing and her jaw sore, and who knew how many other little aches and pains would make themselves known in the next few hours.

She shoved the body aside and untied the remaining rope from around her ankle, flexing it quickly before she rolled to stand on her feet. Time was of the essence. There would be more Russians to deal with, and the ones littering the ground around her would be waking before too long. Except for Alexsei, whose eyes stared blankly at the ceiling.

It was up to her to find Jonah and see if she could put a stop to his insanity. And if she had to save his life to do so, then so be it. She could always kill him after she had the codes to disarm the explosives on the tankers. She was still the best person for the job to find him and corner him like the rabid animal he was.

Audrey leaned down and searched the body nearest to her, relieving him of the gun and knife he'd confiscated from her earlier. Her back was to the door, and though she didn't hear a sound, she knew someone was there—could feel their presence in the shift in the air—and the little prickles of awareness rolled across her skin.

Without warning, she turned and aimed the gun at the intruder. A quirked eyebrow and a cocky grin were all she got in return, and he immediately held his hands up in a sign of peace.

"Don't shoot," he said, the humor still lurking.

She recognized him for what he was—trained to fight. The only question was, who was he fighting for?

He was several inches taller than she was, with the kind of light blond hair that most women could only achieve with a bottle, but she could tell his was perfectly natural. Thick brows were a shade darker in color, and even from where she stood she could see his eyes were as dark as her own. It was an unusual combination. An arresting combination that made her distrust her instincts.

His body was lean and muscled, and he wore black BDUs and a black jacket very similar to her own. He carried himself like a man who was familiar with every aspect of his body, comfortable in his own skin, and confident in what he could do with the muscles beneath.

He was balanced on the balls of his feet and she knew he wouldn't make it easy for her if she decided to fight her way out.

"Well," he said, looking at the scatter of bodies. "This is a hell of a mess. I hope you left at least one of them alive." He started to drop his hands back to his sides.

"Keep your hands up," she demanded, keeping the gun trained on him.

His grin got wider and a flutter of a dimple teased one side of his mouth, but he didn't keep his hands raised. "I've never been very good at following orders. You won't shoot me."

"I just pulled the trigger on a man who probably thought much the same thing. Why is it that men always underestimate what a woman is capable of?"

His face turned serious and a little bit grim. "I've read your file. I would never think of underestimating you." He said it with such conviction she thought he actually might be telling the truth.

"You're agency then," she nodded, as if her suspicions were suddenly confirmed. "I'm not interested in coming back. Sorry you had to make the trip. But you're going to want to get out of my way. I'm in a hurry."

"I guess it's a good thing I'm here to help you. I've been known to move fast from time to time."

"I don't need help. And if you don't move aside I'm going to put a bullet in you just on principle."

"That would make my daughter unhappy. She doesn't like it when I get shot."

Audrey let out a sigh and let the gun drop down to her side. "You're determined to be a pain in the ass, aren't you?"

"I guess that's why my boss sent me for you. Though I don't know what the hell Declan hopes to do with you. And I overheard enough of the conversation between you and your comrades to know you're going to need help. As far as everyone on the planet is concerned, Jonah Salt died in France. You, me, and the Russians are the only ones who know differently. Tracking Jonah Salt won't be a cakewalk. But I can help you."

"You said Declan." Her gaze narrowed on him.

"Declan MacKenzie?"

"Good," he nodded. "It helps speed things up that you've heard of him."

"Of course I've heard of him. Even when I was Mossad I knew who he was. Not to mention he's been trying to track me down for the last year or so. And damned if he's not persistent. He's left messages for me all over hell and back to return his calls. He's a hard man to ignore. But I managed."

"I'll make sure to tell him someone was successful at it," he said dryly.

Her lips wanted to twitch at the obvious good humor on the man's face when he spoke of Declan, but she forced herself to remain impassive. Emotions had no place in the field. That's what had gotten her into trouble the last time.

"Make yourself useful and help me tie them up. I'd like to get at least a little bit of a head start before they come after me."

"I live to serve," he said dryly, but there was such a wicked look of intent in his eyes she had to break contact.

The heat rushed to her cheeks and she figured it was a hell of a time for her body to remember that she was still a woman. It had been three years since she'd had a reaction like that, and she wasn't all that sure it was a welcome feeling. Emotions of any kind distracted from the job. Emotions could get a person killed.

Audrey held the gun on him as he made short work of binding the Russians' hands and feet, and then she made a motion with her weapon for him to move back outside. She leaned down and grabbed her jacket and then followed behind him, keeping her weapon ready just in case her instincts were off and he really was there to kill her. But her gut wasn't tingling, and she thought he might really be there to do as he said.

Once they were outside and a good distance away from the warehouse, he turned and leaned casually against the hood of a Jeep.

"So why did the great Declan MacKenzie send you to find me?" she asked.

"You've just been recruited by MacKenzie Security. Congratulations and welcome to the team. And I wouldn't even consider saying no. If you know Dec's reputation then you know he pretty much always gets what he wants. I'm sure there's some kind of paperwork you'll need to fill out. Life insurance policies and all that," he said, grinning. "But as of this moment you're on payroll, so it's probably a good thing you only killed one of those

Russians."

Audrey narrowed her eyes and tried to sift through all the possible scenarios of what could happen. And then she decided maybe she could use this man's help after all. At least for a little while. MacKenzie Security had a hell of a lot of power and unlimited resources.

"Do you have a name, or are you just Declan MacKenzie's mouthpiece?"

"Archer Ryan," he said, holding out a hand for her to shake. "And sweetheart, I'm nobody's mouthpiece."

Before Audrey had time to blink he moved in fast, twisting the gun out of her hand. She countered the move, pivoting in the opposite direction. Their bodies were close enough that she could feel the heat of his body as they went through the dance of close combat. He hit the small button on the side of the gun while she still held it and the magazine dropped into his hand. He pulled back the slide and ejected the bullet, letting it fall silently into the snow. Both of her arms were restrained and she was left defenseless—not unless she wanted to really hurt him—and the entire time he never once took his eyes from hers.

Her breath came in short pants as she felt the

familiar connection between a man and a woman—the tingles of attraction that pebbled the skin and heated the blood. She felt the blood drain from her face and she immediately released her hold on the gun and fought to get out of his grasp. She wanted no part of any connection unless it helped her reach her goal of finding Jonah.

Archer immediately let her go and looked at her curiously. He held the gun out to her, butt end first. "You ready to go?" he asked as if nothing was out of the normal.

Audrey took the gun and then held her hand out for the magazine, wondering if he'd give it to her. He placed it in her hand, looking at her with those dark eyes, and trusting her not to kill him. She wasn't sure if she could've done the same. So she took the magazine and popped it back in before returning the weapon to the small of her back.

And then she did what she'd swore she'd never do again—take on another partner. "Let's go."

CHAPTER FIVE

Shane MacKenzie was finished. Finished with hospitals and the nurses who looked at him with sympathy instead of the flirtatious glances he was used to getting from women. He was sick of the doctors and the blood tests. And most of all, he was fucking *sick* of physical therapy.

They'd had him up and moving around for the last three weeks, giving him pats on the back and pushing him on with excitement tinged voices filled with false encouragement, like he was a fucking kid learning how to ride a bike for the first time.

The humiliation of having to be propped up and coddled every step of the way burned in his guts until he wanted to put his fist through the damned wall. They told him he'd have to use the crutches until he was ready to be fit for a prosthetic. The swelling in his leg hadn't gone down as they'd hoped yet, so the process had been delayed. His other leg was whole, but every time he put his full weight down it felt as if someone was driving a hot poker through the bottom of his foot and up his leg.

But they still yelled encouragement and made him walk on it. And because he didn't want to disappoint his family—who always managed to show up when he'd prefer to be alone—he gritted his teeth and did what he was told. And he hated it. Hated each and every one of those people smiling at him and pushing him forward.

They told him he was lucky because his body was strong and that would help him get back to a hundred percent faster. But he knew he'd never be a hundred percent again. Every word of praise out of their mouths was a fucking lie and he was sick of it all. He wanted to be left alone.

Shane ripped the medical tape from the back of his hand and pulled out the IV, tossing it on the bed. He pulled off the pulse monitor on his finger, not caring that the little machine by his head started the incessant beeping that drove him insane.

He lowered the bed rail and tossed back the covers. It still took him by surprise to see empty space where his leg should have been. They'd cut one leg off of his sweats so he wouldn't trip on the flapping cloth during PT, and a white bandaged stub was all that could be seen. His heart pumped a little faster at the reminder, and the anger that had been festering the last couple of weeks since he'd started physical therapy made his hands shake with rage.

His crutches rested against the wall near his bed, not close enough to reach out and grab, but surely he could manage to hobble a few steps to reach them. And then he was going to put clothes on and catch the first cab out of this place. He was done.

He tossed his legs over the side of the bed, and already beads of sweat were breaking out over his skin at the exertion. God, if his fucking SEAL team could see him now they'd probably laugh their asses off at how weak he was.

A sock covered his remaining foot and he placed it on the floor, putting a little bit of his weight on it. His fingers dug into the side of the bed but he pushed through and stood, wobbling like a newborn colt as he tried to manage his pain. That's what they kept telling him, over and over again. That he just needed to learn how to manage his pain. Well it was a lot fucking easier to manage the pain with the Percocet they doled out so stingily.

He held himself steady using the bedrail for support and held his other hand out toward the wall, stretching to see if he could reach the crutches without having to move. Sweat dripped from his brow with the exertion and his skin felt as if it were being stretched over a hot flame.

Shane hobbled on his good foot, each bounce making the pins in his leg feel like knives. He tasted blood and realized he'd bitten the inside of his cheek to keep quiet through the pain. His fingers brushed the top of one of the crutches and he almost laughed with relief.

"Come on, come on," he whispered. His fingers nudged the crutch again, pulling it forward so he could catch it. But just as it fell forward his leg gave out. There was no warning. One moment he was standing and the next he was on the ground, the crutches falling to land on top of him as if by some cruel joke.

"Goddammit!" He threw the crutch closest to him at the wall, taking out a lamp and a potted plant that the nurses insisted on watering every damned day. Tears of frustration and pain filled his eyes and he rolled to his side. He took the other crutch and slammed it against the equipment placed around his bed, toppling carts and stands to the ground. At least he still had strength somewhere in his body.

"Oh, God. Shane."

The voice of his mother had him pulling back his temper, but *God*, he wished she'd just go away. She gasped and he realized he'd said the words out loud. He immediately felt shitty for saying it, and it wasn't like he could take the words back.

"Go away. Leave me alone," he said softly.

"Mom," Declan came in the room behind her and put a hand on her shoulder, holding her back from rushing to her youngest son. "Go grab a cup of coffee for a minute or two."

"Dec." She shook her head in warning, looking back and forth between her boys.

"Go, Mom. It'll be fine. I promise."

"Both of you just get the fuck out!" he screamed, rolling to his stomach so he could prop himself up, though he probably looked like a fish out of water, flopping around on the damned floor.

"Don't you talk to me like that, Shane MacKenzie. I don't care how hurt you are. I raised you better than that." His mother's voice was like a whip against his skin and he could hear the hurt he'd caused.

"I'm sorry, Mom." He dropped his head to the

carpet and tried to catch his breath. "I really am. But please go for a little while."

He heard the door close and used his arms to push himself up to face his brother. He knew Dec well enough to know that he'd go as soon as he damn well felt like it. Nothing and no one pushed Dec around, especially his brothers. Well, maybe Cade, but that's only because Cade was the oldest and had a head as hard as a rock and a black temper to go with it. Though he'd mellowed considerably since he'd become a husband and a father.

"How stubborn are you going to be about this?" Dec asked, coming closer. "Are you going to insist on doing this yourself or will you let me help you?"

Shane turned his head and looked at his brother. There was no judgment in Declan's eyes. No pity or sympathy. His face was as impassive as always.

"If you want to help you'll get me the hell out of this place. I want to go home to my own bed and own space. I'm tired of being poked and prodded. I just want everyone to leave me alone."

"All right then," Dec said. "I'll make it happen if you promise to keep seeing the physical therapist when she makes house calls."

"You need to leave me alone right now, Dec. Go make whatever calls you have to and get me out, but leave me the hell alone before I hurt you or someone else. I'm not fit for company at the moment."

Shane continued to push himself to a sitting position and then he grabbed hold of the bedrails, his muscles straining as he lifted himself back up into the bed. "And as you can see, I can take care of myself."

"So it appears," Dec conceded. "But I'll be damned if any of us are going to leave you alone like you want. Get mad. Throw a couple of punches at me and Cade and Grant if it'll make you feel better. It's nothing we can't handle. And you probably deserve a fist in the jaw for the look you just put on Mom's face."

Shane collapsed against the bed, his skin and sweats soaked with perspiration, and he closed his eyes against the frustration and anger that hadn't found an outlet yet.

"I apologized," he said, the guilt eating at him. "But why can't you fucking listen? I said go away and leave me the hell alone. I've had it up to my eyeballs with MacKenzies."

"I'll go get the release paperwork started, but

I'll be back. You're stuck with us whether you want us or not. You've been a MacKenzie all your life, so you know none of us are going anywhere."

"Fucking fantastic. Close the door behind you."

Dec headed back to the door and started to pull it closed on his way out. But he stopped and stuck his head back in. "I'm glad you're angry, Shane. You want to know why?"

"Not really, but I'm sure you're going to tell me."

Dec grunted in what might have been amusement. "Angry means you're not dead. Maybe you should think about that."

CHAPTER SIX

Cold winds blew bitterly, cutting straight through the body and into the soul. Still, Audrey preferred the Alaska cold over Russia any day of the week. There was a wild, untamed beauty about the land that inspired a mix of awe, fear, and respect.

Rolling hills of white went for as far as the eye could see, and in the background were snowy mountains that peaked straight into the clouds. Frozen rivers and streams jutted off in all directions, and she bet it was beautiful once the weather warmed and there was color. But for now it was a frozen palace of snow and ice, isolating and eerily quiet in its solitude.

There was nothing *but* solitude.

"This isn't going to be easy," she said as Archer retraced their route back to the docks where she'd been taken—where she'd fired the shot at Jonah. "There's so much empty space here. It's the perfect place to disappear. And it's snowing again. If we don't hurry all the tracks will be gone."

"It's hard to disappear with a bullet wound and dripping blood everywhere. We'll find him."

Audrey hadn't relaxed since she'd gotten in the car with him, and it had only been a phone call to Declan MacKenzie himself that had assured her that Archer Ryan was exactly who he said he was. But still...the car ride had been filled with uncomfortable silence, and she'd sat coiled and ready for whatever awaited her.

"You were lovers," Archer said after a few more minutes of silence. "You and Salt."

"That's none of your business. We should be getting close to the docks. I was only in the car for an hour or so."

"I told you I read your file." He completely ignored her attempt to change the subject and her shoulders tensed as she sat up straighter in the passenger seat. "It doesn't take much deductive work to figure out from the way you were found and your medicals that you were closer than partners. And now that I know he's alive, I can deduce that he's the one who shot you. That's fucking cold. No wonder you're out for blood."

"Thank you, Agent Ryan, for that analysis," she said, her voice as frigid and brittle as the wind outside.

She heard his sigh and ran through scenarios of how he could use the information against her. In their line of work, information was power.

"I just want you to know I understand what it took for you to come with me. To agree to work with someone again. Fuck Jonah Salt. He's got his own agenda and never intended to utilize your talents. His only thought was to use you how he saw fit. But he underestimated the agent you are."

Audrey turned to look at him and found his dark gaze steady and intent on hers. There it was again. That connection that inexplicably linked two people who'd never met and made it seem like they'd known each other forever. He was the one that broke the spell this time as he focused back on the road.

"If he'd bothered to read your file from front to back, he'd have known what a mistake it was to let you live once he'd gotten the word you'd survived his first attempt to kill you. Your profile suggests you don't quit until the job is done. It's you who's going to stop him in the end. I believe that with every instinct in my body."

If Audrey had the ability to cry, she might have in that moment. She felt the burn behind her eyes, but no tears formed. She hadn't felt anything but hate since she'd died on that operating table. It had been too long since she'd been around people, and she realized how she must seem to someone like Archer Ryan.

He seemed to be fairly laid back with an easy temperament who took situations as they came, but was able to assess them quickly. She hadn't seen how he worked yet and she didn't know his skills, other than his quick display back at the warehouse, but she knew the reputation of MacKenzie Security. Declan MacKenzie only hired the best agents, so Archer, whatever his skills, was no slacker and he wasn't someone to underestimate.

To him, she probably seemed like a stone cold bitch. A loose cannon if ever there was one. And if she'd been Archer, she'd wonder why the hell his boss was sending him on a wild goose chase to recruit an agent who was hell bent on vengeance.

But she was still human. And though she didn't want them, she had feelings and understood that he was extending an olive branch of sorts. She wasn't cold, and she missed human contact.

"Thank you," she said softly. And that was all that had to be said. She relaxed and felt the tension leave her shoulders as they made the rest of the drive to the docks.

It was past noon by the time Archer parked the Jeep at the edge of the docks. The snow was falling harder now and they had maybe an hour before all tracks were covered.

There was no sign of the Russians, so they'd probably come and gone. The longer she and Archer spent retracing their steps, the farther behind Jonah they'd be, and it wouldn't be long before more Russian agents appeared.

"The docks are pretty deserted," Archer said, grabbing a pair of binoculars to look further down the shoreline.

Audrey saw the tanker in the distance where she'd taken the shot at Jonah. It had traveled a good distance, but was still visible to the naked eye. She knew now there was an explosive device somewhere underneath.

"That's the tanker where I found Jonah this morning."

"We'll leave it as is for now. Jonah probably

has sensors near the explosives and we don't want him to detonate if he thinks there's a team down there trying to disarm it. I'll pass the information along to Declan and let him make the call. Come on. Let's go see if anyone remembers seeing anything."

Gray clouds grew thicker as the snow fell—bulging and obese, they looked as if their seams were ready to split and dump white powder over the entire town until it was buried to the rooftops. She pulled a black ski cap over her hair and realized there was nothing she could do to cover the bruise forming on the side of her face. It throbbed like a bitch, but there was nothing to be done for it.

"I wouldn't mind paying a visit to that little fishershit Jerry that sold me out to the Russians," she said, narrowing her eyes.

"Damn, woman. If you could see your face right now." Archer grinned and pulled on his own watch cap and then the hood of his jacket over that. "I'd be shaking in my fisherboots if I was him."

She groaned before she could help it and rolled her eyes. "You can't be for real. Declan MacKenzie would not hire an idiot for his team."

"Just remember that, sweetheart, and we'll be good to go. I've learned in this business you have to take your pleasures where you can. Otherwise you'll burn out and end up eating your own bullet."

Archer grabbed a pistol from beneath his seat and got out of the Jeep, putting it at the small of his back, and she did the same.

"Oh, and Archer." Audrey waited until he turned to give her his full attention. "The next time you call me sweetheart I'm going to put a bullet in your kneecap. I'm not a fan of endearments." Not since Jonah Salt had used them so freely.

"Make sure you shoot for my left knee. The cartilage is already worn to shit and I've heard the R&D lab at MacKenzie Security can give me a new bionic one."

He turned away from her and started walking toward the docks. Audrey blew out a breath. She had no idea how to handle Archer Ryan, and it was disturbing to say the least.

"Shit," she said under her breath and followed after him.

Her eyes were never still, tracking the roads and possible hiding places where Jonah or the Russians could be waiting to ambush them. Archer had been right. The docks were all but deserted at this time of the day, but there was a kid of about nineteen or twenty looping rope in a figure eight pattern around two wooden posts up on a boat.

"Hey, man," Archer called out. "Can I talk to you for a minute?"

The kid looked up from his ropes. His face was pockmarked with acne scars and a red bandana was tied around his head to keep his long hair out of his eyes.

"Time's money, man." And then he went back to his rope.

"So it is." Archer pulled out his wallet and a couple of twenties and the kid let the rope fall. He jumped over the side of the boat and landed in front of them on the dock with the surefootedness of someone who spent most of their time at sea. He held out his hand for the money.

"Information first," Archer said, making the kid grin and shrug. "How long have you been hanging around today?"

"My old man and me take tourists out for fishing. We had clients this morning that paid big bucks to wake up early and freeze their asses off just so they could take a picture with a fish half their size and hang it in an office on Wall Street somewhere. But we had to cancel the trip and reschedule for tomorrow.

"Denny, he's the police chief. He came by with a few other cops and said a couple tourists saw a lady get kidnapped this morning. The tourists were making a stink about it so Denny and the others made all the boats stay docked so they could search them for the woman."

"Did they find her?"

"Nah, it was bogus. Old Jerry told them they was crazy. That's his boat down there," he said, pointing to the boat Audrey had taken out that morning to search for Jonah. Her face didn't betray her feelings. It wasn't the kid's fault old Jerry was a two-timing asshole.

"Jerry told them it must have been a crank call cause nothing but fishing and tourist type stuff goes on down at these docks. We all make our living from the water, and a day wasted is money gone. Which is why if you want more information you're going to have to add another twenty."

Archer peeled off two more twenties and a picture out of the inside pocket of his jacket. "Did you happen to see this man hanging around this morning? It's possible he was hurt."

The kid stared at the photo and then shrugged.

"I don't know man, it was dark. Only thing weird I saw this morning was a yellow Zodiac heading north up the shoreline. Didn't pay much attention to it. Figured it might have been one of the guys unloading some drugs or something before the cops boarded the boats. We've got cargo planes going in and out all the time bringing shit in and taking it out again. I wouldn't be surprised if not all of it was legal."

Archer passed over the money. "I don't suppose old Jerry is still around for the day?"

"Nah, dude went home sick after the cops left. Didn't look good at all. He's a drunk, so I figure he had a bad night."

"Thanks for your help, man." The kid scurried up the rope ladder and was back on deck before they'd turned to walk away.

"Lucky for old Jerry he got sick," Audrey said as they headed back toward the Jeep.

"Let's follow the north road for as long as we can and see if we can find the Zodiac. He'll have dumped it and had a contingency plan of some kind. You know he was here almost twenty-four hours before you arrived."

They got back in the Jeep and he started it up,

backtracking the way they'd come and following the coast road that would eventually dead end. All of the roads out of Nome led to nowhere. It was well and truly isolated unless you had means to traverse the land in other ways.

"What will he do next?" Archer asked. "Tell me your gut feeling."

He'd do exactly what Audrey was afraid he might do. He was going to disappear. "He's wounded, but he won't need help. He's trained in medical and he'll know what to do to patch himself up. You're right. He was here long enough to gather supplies and set up transportation. He'd have to do it here in town though, so we can check that out if we lose his trail. He's going to disappear right in front of our faces. He'll use the land and his skills to live until he thinks it's safe to head somewhere else."

"Don't forget the Russians," Archer said. "We're not the only ones looking for him. And they're going to be looking for *us* too. Salt is going to need access to the Internet, otherwise his blackmail scheme isn't going to work. And as much as we like to think it isn't so, technology is the best way to find someone."

"Say we find Jonah. How are we going to

disarm the bombs on those tankers without him blowing them first? He'll have detonation codes and there's no way in hell he'll be giving them to us. "

"That's the million dollar question, sweet—" Archer looked at her sheepishly out of the corner of his eye and grinned. "Agent Sharpe."

"And your bionic knee is put on hold another day." She felt her lips twitch and looked out the window to hide it.

"In all seriousness, when we get to that point, that's when you're going to be glad MacKenzie Security is on your side. Cal Colter is one of the best computer hackers I've ever seen. It makes the CIA and the Pentagon really nervous that he's working for Declan and not in house."

"Never heard of him," she said.

"Most people only know of him as Cypher."

"Right," Audrey said, impressed. "Him I've heard of." And the fact that MacKenzie Security had acquired someone who was considered as much of a threat as a hero for all the good he'd done for the country said something. Cypher was a man of many talents. It only made her more curious about the man sitting next to her and what he was hiding.

"Look there," he said, pulling to the side of the

road. "Tracks in the snow. Multiple sets by the looks of it."

He left the engine running and they both got out, leaving the doors open in case they needed cover. Audrey's gun was out and she automatically covered Archer's back as they looked around for any unseen threats. The land was open and there wasn't a good place for cover, so they both relaxed and focused on the tracks that were quickly being filled in.

"Blood," Archer said, bending down in the road to get a closer look.

"He tried to cover his tracks, sweeping behind himself, but he took a direct hit. There's no way he didn't leave blood behind. Looks like we found where he came back on land."

"And there's the Zodiac."

There was a steep drop from the road to the shoreline and Archer stood right at the edge looking down. The Zodiac, or what was left of it, rippled like ribbons in the water, caught on some kind of plant. Jonah had taken his knife to it to help it sink faster, but it would've still been dark when he'd come ashore and he'd have been in a hurry.

"He's making mistakes," she said. "He could

be hurt worse than I thought."

"If he's made one, he'll make others. He had some kind of vehicle parked here on the road so he could get out easily."

"It looks like a snowmobile or something similar. The tracks are odd. The other set of tires are going to be from our Russian friends."

"Let's follow the trail for as long as we can, then we'll need to stop and regroup and pick up some supplies. I'll need to check in with Declan too."

Audrey looked over at him and arched a brow. "And how are your survivalist skills, Agent Ryan?"

He went back to the Jeep, but she saw his mouth twitch. "They're passable. You won't have to haul me through the snow on your back, if that's what you're wondering."

"Don't worry. I'd just leave you to the scavengers. Wolves get awful hungry this time of year." She had to admit she enjoyed bantering with him. And he might not know it, but if she had to she'd haul him out of hell. Because that's what partners did. And until he proved otherwise, that's just what he was, and she'd already begun to think of him that way.

"You have a mean streak," he said, putting the Jeep in drive and following the tracks left in the road. "I don't know why I like that about you."

The laugh took her by surprise. It had been so long since she'd done it she almost didn't recognize the sound that had come from her throat.

"You know, neither you or Declan mentioned what your background was. Were you military or CIA? I don't remember ever hearing the name Archer Ryan whispered among the legends."

"What can I say, I'm a private kind of guy."

"Declan MacKenzie always worked with the same team. Cypher was one of those people. Gabe Brennan was another."

"Gabe Brennan has opened his own security agency on the European side of things. He and Dec still work together on occasion."

"Kane Huxley was also in his band of merry men."

"Yeah, well, Kane Huxley turned out to be as big a bastard as Jonah Salt. You're not the only one who's been betrayed by someone you thought you could trust. By a friend you've known most of your life. Declan and Sophia are lucky to be alive."

Audrey tilted her head and looked closely at him. He didn't give anything away. There was no emotion on his face. No outward signs that he was uncomfortable talking about the subject. But her gut told her there was more there than he was letting on.

"If I recall, the fifth man on Dec's team was a guy named Warlock. I don't recall ever hearing what happened to him. Does he work for MacKenzie Security?"

Archer braked and brought the Jeep to an easy stop in the road. Visibility was becoming more difficult by the second and the tracks had all but disappeared. They were going to have to stop and turn back until things cleared up.

She kept looking at him, waiting for— something. Something that would give her a clue about the man she was entrusting her life to.

He put the Jeep in reverse and did a 3-point turn to take them back into town, but he stopped and looked at her, his face unusually serious. She hadn't really realized until that moment how his face had always been filled with such good humor. She wondered now if it was a mask to hide something darker.

"You know him?" She finally asked, after the tension dragged on.

SIZZLE

He shook his head and turned back to the road. "Never heard of him."

CHAPTER SEVEN

The Jeep crept along the road and the windows strained as the wind blew off the water, and Archer kept his grip relaxed against the wheel, despite the pounding need in him to squeeze it hard enough to make his hands ache.

He had no idea what had just happened, but Audrey Sharpe was more perceptive than he'd given her credit for. Just because she'd isolated herself the last couple of years didn't mean she'd forgotten how to read someone.

It had been years since he'd heard the name Warlock—for good reason. Warlock had been killed in Russia. And because Warlock had died, Archer Ryan had been able to live out in the open and without fear that someone would try to hunt him down. Cypher had made sure that all mentions of Warlock and Archer Ryan being one and same had been erased from history. It was still possible his past could catch up to him at some point, but it was unlikely. Cypher was the best.

Warlock had seen and done things for his country that still ate holes in his gut if he thought about them too long. The memories still plagued him in nightmares, which was part of the reason his sex life wasn't nearly as exciting as Declan's. Most women didn't care to be woken out of a sound sleep by a man screaming as if being skinned alive by Satan himself.

He'd have to be very careful with Audrey and make sure she didn't find out the truth about the monster he'd been, and why it had been so important for him to die and start over again.

Snow blew so hard into the windshield that it was impossible to see anything but white, so Archer almost hit the man standing in the middle of the road before he saw him. He slammed on the brakes and was thankful he hadn't been going very fast to begin with. Audrey had her gun out and pointed at the windshield before he'd come to a complete stop.

Archer was about to slam the car in reverse when the man's hands came up in front of him, palms out in a gesture to signal they stop. A heavy coat lined with fur dwarfed him, and a fur-lined hood surrounded his face. And then between swishes of the wipers, he was gone as quickly as he appeared.

"What the hell—" Audrey said, bringing her gun down.

The knock on Archer's window had both of their weapons coming up and their adrenaline spiking. The old man's face was all but pressed up to the glass, brown and wrinkled with age, most of his teeth missing as he smiled a jack-o-lantern smile. Snow gathered on his eyebrows and lashes and gray hair hung in long braids on both sides of his face. Archer released the breath he'd been holding and put his gun in his lap, though he kept his hand on it.

"Holy shit," Audrey said, releasing her own breath. "That was creepy. What the hell does he want?"

"Let's find out." He rolled down the window and snow blew into the car, slapping and stinging against his face.

"Declan MacKenzie sent me," the old man said, his native accent thick but not difficult to understand. He eyed the gun Audrey pointed at him with curiosity and then turned back to Archer, dismissing the threat. "I'll ride in back and you can take me to town. This weather is a bitch, and I'm old."

No kidding, Archer thought. The man had to be about the oldest person he'd ever seen. He sighed and hit the lock switch so the man could get in.

The man moved to the back door and Archer whispered, "Of course Declan sent him. Only Declan would send the oldest man in the universe to help us. He's probably sitting at home, laughing his ass off."

"Declan doesn't strike me as the type of guy to have much of a sense of humor," Audrey said.

She watched the man closely as he got into the backseat, and Archer noticed she didn't take her weapon off him, though she did relax her grip some.

"Oh, Declan is a very funny guy," the man said, nodding. "Prankster."

"That's very true," Archer said. "Why did Declan send you?"

"He said you need supplies. I have supplies." The man shrugged and threw his hands up, sending droplets of water throughout the car. "Simple fix. You will stay with me until the storm clears. My name is Chanlyeya, but everyone calls me Joe."

Archer knew when to not argue, and he'd stopped questioning long ago how Declan knew before his agents did when they were going to need something. He had contingency plans on top of contingency plans.

"The man you are after will not get far. The storm is too bad. And the two men after him will not get far either. Plenty of time. I am wise and old. You will listen to me. You hungry?"

"I could eat," Archer said, pressing on the gas pedal.

"You drive like an old woman," Joe said. "We'll not get there until tonight. Pedal to the metal, friend. I'll be your eyes."

Archer gritted his teeth and ignored Audrey's snicker from the passenger seat. So *now* she decided to get her sense of humor back. He did the only thing he could to save face and pushed on the gas, the Jeep fishtailing once before righting itself and speeding ahead.

Strangely enough, using Joe's eyes worked pretty well and Archer just followed his directions until they got back to town.

"Stop here," Joe said. "No point in going

further. You won't be using a car again for many days. The snow will cover them all by morning."

"It's too bad Jonah didn't choose Key West for this little adventure," Audrey muttered under her breath. "I wouldn't mind a little sun and sand right about now."

"I was in Afghanistan for a while. Sand is overrated if there isn't a beach there to accompany it. I've probably still got sand in places I don't care to mention."

"Maybe one day you'll find a pearl in your shorts," Joe said, grinning a gap-toothed grin.

This time Audrey laughed out loud and slapped her hand over her mouth to keep it inside. Archer could tell she'd surprised herself by the action, and if he could give her that then he'd let Joe make fun of him all he wanted.

"Is your house close?" he asked, pushing open the car door and stepping out into the wind and snow.

"Close enough." Joe pulled the hood back up over his braids, but he didn't seem to be bothered by the cold.

Audrey's lips were pressed tight together as she tried to keep her teeth from chattering. She zipped her jacket up to her neck and pulled her hat low. They were going to need more gear if they were going to follow Jonah across Alaska. She hoped Joe could do as he'd promised Declan.

Archer retrieved his duffel bag from the back and realized Audrey didn't have anything but the weapons on her. As if reading his mind she said, "I stashed my pack down by the docks and the Russians took my rifle."

He nodded and then they followed Joe the rest of the way into town, hunched over and going head first into the wind, the snow relentless as it seemed to grow beneath their feet. They reached the end of a long narrow street. There wasn't another person in sight—only squat buildings in various sizes with flat roofs that flanked each side of the narrow lane.

It was a surreal feeling standing on a street that felt as if it were the jumping off place for the end of the earth. The snowflakes were fast and furious, flying down the narrow lane and heading straight for them as if they were being projected through a wind tunnel. It was terrifyingly beautiful, and he took a moment to just stand and watch nature rage around him.

Audrey's hand on his arm had him looking down at her, and he was struck again as he had been the first time he'd looked at her photograph. He decided it had to be her eyes that cast him under her spell. They were big and dark and exotically tilted at the corners. She wore no makeup, but her lashes were long and black and it looked as if she'd lined her eyes with liner, but he knew it was natural.

Her face was paper white because of the cold and her lips void of any color. But still she was the most beautiful woman he'd ever set eyes on.

"Are you all right?" she asked softly and then dropped her hand back to her side.

"I'm fine." He mentally shook himself out of the trance and busied himself looking anywhere but at her. She was dangerous. And she was still an unknown variable as far as the job was concerned. "I just had one of those moments where everything lined up exactly how it was supposed to."

She nodded as if she knew what he was talking about. Hell, maybe she did.

"Those moments are part of the reason I like working alone. When the world comes into sharp focus and you can practically feel the silence living inside of you. Moments like that are rare."

It seemed she knew what he was talking about after all.

"Hey. Chatterboxes. Come, come," Joe said,

waving them forward.

The house was right on the corner and didn't seem to be much bigger than an overgrown dollhouse. The roof over the wide front porch sagged dangerously beneath the weight of the snow, but Joe didn't seem overly concerned about it collapsing on him.

Navigating the stairs to the front door was a challenge. Archer caught Audrey's arm and held her up against his body when she stepped into the empty space between the steps.

He held on to her until she found her footing and he realized at that point that it had been much too long since he'd had a woman that close to him. His body responded despite him standing in the equivalent of an ice shower, and he was grateful all the layers hid the throbbing erection pulsing behind the zipper of his cargos. It was a fine time for his libido to rediscover itself, that was for damned sure.

He'd spent the last few years working almost non-stop, and he was past the age where finding any willing woman was enough. He wasn't a monk, but he'd stopped thinking he could have a normal life outside of the agency. Audrey Sharpe was blowing those thoughts all to hell.

The siding of the house was bright green, and

two square windows not big enough for a body to fit through flanked each side of a peeling wood door. Joe pushed against the door, swollen with age and damp, and they all shuffled into a cozy room with a blazing fire that took up almost the entire wall to their left.

One room was all it was, and Archer figured he could touch both sides if he held his arms straight out. A wood table and two chairs were pushed against the wall and a little kitchenette was set up in the corner.

A woman at least as old as Joe was stirring something that smelled good enough to have Archer's stomach rumbling loudly, and her smile lit up her face as they came in, making Archer think she must have been a very pretty woman in her youth.

She hustled over and spoke to Joe quickly in their native tongue, and then Joe looked to them for introductions.

"This is my wife, Ahnah. She says to hang your coats on the pegs and take these blankets over by the fire and strip out of your clothes. She will wash and dry them for you before your journey."

He shoved two heavy blankets at them and gave them a shove. Archer ducked his head to hide his grin at Audrey's perplexed look, but she followed him over to the fireplace while Joe and Ahnah huddled in the kitchen area, whispering softly to each other.

Archer unfolded the blanket and saw it was more than large enough to cover him from head to toe, so he wrapped it around his shoulders and then turned his back before stripping out of his clothes and boots. The sounds of Audrey doing the same behind him weren't helping matters below his waist. His cock was rigid and aching, and the worst possible thing he could do was let her know how attracted he was to her. She'd run like a scared rabbit. And he couldn't blame her one bit.

He wanted to get his hands on Jonah Salt for what he'd done to her, and every time he thought about the level of betrayal it took to be intimate with someone and then shoot them in cold blood, it made him boil with hatred for a man he'd never met. And if Audrey didn't kill Salt, then *he* would.

Archer wrapped the blanket so it covered him completely and turned toward the fire. Audrey looked completely uncomfortable and out of her element. She was probably thinking being naked was going to be pretty inconvenient if they'd walked into a trap and she needed to start running.

He'd already had the same thought and had

made sure he'd palmed his weapons and hidden them beneath the blanket when it had been handed to him. He scooted closer to Audrey, so they stood shoulder to shoulder in front of the fire, the wool blankets itchy but warm, and he passed her an extra handgun so Joe and Ahnah couldn't see.

Some of the tension left her shoulders and she looked up at him with a half smile as she hid it quickly beneath her own blanket.

"That obvious, huh?"

"I just figured if I was worried about it, you probably were too."

They stood in uncomfortable silence for a few minutes, the heat building between them in ways that had nothing to do with the fire. At least it was on his end. He had no idea what was going on inside her head, and he wondered if the connection between them was only one sided.

He'd never been the kind of man to hold back when he was attracted to a woman. But she was different. She'd been hurt in unimaginable ways, and he realized he'd never put himself in the position of being another person to add to that hurt.

"This would be a really awkward situation if this were a first date," he said to break the silence.

Her eyes got bigger, as if she wasn't quite sure how to respond, but then she said, "I've never actually been on a date, so I wouldn't know."

She'd spoken so softly he wasn't sure he'd heard her correctly, and he froze, unsure of what to say next.

"Never?" he finally asked. "In all the relationships you've had, none of them has taken you out on a date?"

Audrey turned those big brown eyes on him and her mouth quirked a little. "It's not like there's a lot of time for that kind of stuff in this line of work. You don't just slit a Jordanian Prince's throat and run off to the movies and share popcorn. You work and you have sex because the body needs it. There's no time for anything in between. And I think it's wasted anyway."

"I'm sorry. Did you just say romance was a waste of time?" Their heads had gotten closer together and their whispers more fervent, and he realized things were heating up pretty damned fast and he was going to have to go back outside and stand in the snow to cool off. "Why do I feel like there's an odd gender reversal going on here?"

"Is that your way of saying you're a woman?" she asked, arching a brow.

Their bodies moved even closer, so his breath whispered across her skin, and he saw by the widening of her eyes that she wasn't completely unaffected by the close contact.

"You want to be careful, sweetheart, about biting off more than you can chew here."

"Did you just call me sweetheart?" Her eyes narrowed, and if he'd been less of a man, in that moment his balls would have shriveled to the size of acorns.

"Don't even try it. You and I both know I could disarm you before you took aim. Don't play games you don't intend to follow through with."

They'd gone from playful banter to something much more serious in the blink of an eye, and he moved back a step to let things cool down.

"And it just so happens I like going on dates. And I'd have no problem doing my job and then taking you out somewhere afterward."

"Are you asking me out?" The color had drained from her face and she took another step away from him, as if she'd just realized where the conversation was leading. "Oh, no. No, no, no. Definitely not."

"You forgot *non, nein,* and *ne*. Three of my

favorite languages."

"My job is to kill Jonah Salt. Nothing else is more important than that. He killed any possible feelings I could ever have for a man again."

"Forever is a long time. It seems shortsighted to think you wouldn't have those desires at some point during the rest of your life."

"If I do, then I'll deal with it. But I promise that part of me is as dead as Jonah is going to be."

"That sounds like a challenge, Agent Sharpe. And if you're so determined to have sex before going out on a date, I could probably be persuaded to accommodate you."

"You're bound and determined for me to shoot you, aren't you?"

He cracked out a laugh and shook his head, enjoying their short conversation more than he'd expected. A small smile tilted the corner of her lips and he realized she might not trust him—*yet*—but she accepted him as her partner. The other things would come over time.

"Hey," Joe called out. "Chatterboxes. You want to   eat?"

CHAPTER EIGHT

Audrey sat at the little two-person table and huddled over the fish stew Ahnah had ladled into heavy ceramic bowls. Archer sat across from her—she'd stopped trying to figure out how to keep their knees from bumping beneath the table—and she settled in and tried not to think about what that small bit of physical contact made her feel.

She'd lied when she'd told him that part of her body—the sexual urges she'd never been ashamed of before—had died when Jonah had tried to kill her. Those feelings had only been dead until she'd met Archer Ryan. And he was right, she'd bitten off more than she could chew where he was concerned.

Ahnah had gone upstairs to where Audrey presumed the bedroom and bathroom were located.

At least she hoped they had a bathroom. Walking to an outhouse in this weather would be on par with walking through the fires of hell.

Joe pulled a rocking chair closer to the fire and watched them eat in unnerving silence.

"So how do you know Declan?" Archer asked. Apparently the silence was getting to him too.

"Oh," Joe shrugged. "We go back. Secret lives and younger days. Declan's one of the good guys. He tells me you are too, so I help him."

"Did he tell you who we're looking for?"

"Didn't have to." Joe pulled a pipe from the front pocket of his shirt and used the wood of the chair leg to strike his match. He held the flame to the pipe and puffed greedily, his cheeks hollowing as a thin plume of smoke rose from the bowl. He exhaled and a white cloud of pungent smoke filled the room.

"Men come and men go in our corner of the world. And the land eats those who are not strong enough to survive. The man you chase is strong, yes?" The rocker creaked as he went back and forth, the sound almost hypnotic.

Audrey's spoon hit the bottom of her bowl and she realized she'd been hungrier than she thought.

She was warm and full, and so she settled back against the wall to listen to Joe.

"No offense, Joe." Archer hit the bottom of his own bowl and leaned back against the wall with his arms crossed over his chest. "But if Dec has sent us to you because you're some magical shaman who sees the future in your pipe smoke, I'm going to disappoint you and say we're not interested."

Joe wheezed out a laugh, his rocker coming forward as his feet hit the floor, and he slapped his hand on his thigh. "Boy, there's nothing in this smoke except weed. The medicinal kind," he said, winking. "Helps with my arthritis."

Joe took another puff and started rocking again. "Truth is, my wife is from here and so were my grandparents, but I was actually born and raised in Minnetonka."

"So why the mysterious appearing in the middle of a blizzard in the road routine?" Audrey asked.

"It freaks people out, and I find people see exactly what they want to see when they look at me," he said grinning, showing the gaps in his teeth. As if he'd flipped a switch his speech went from the stilted English of a Native to the distinct twang of Minnesota.

Joe's eyes sparkled with laughter and Audrey found herself smiling with him. It had been a long while since she'd enjoyed herself quite so much.

"If you didn't want everyone to know you're in town, you shouldn't have questioned Zeke Marley over at the docks. That kid couldn't keep a secret if a gun was held to his head. Everyone in town knows you're looking for a wounded man and that it has something to do with the woman those tourists say was kidnapped this morning. Denny— our chief of police—knows something funny is going on, but there's no proof of anything other than rumor."

"Where would a wounded man go to hide in a storm like this one?"

"That depends on the man." Joe snuffed out his pipe and put it back in his shirt pocket a few seconds before Ahnah came back down the stairs.

Audrey guessed by the narrow-eyed gaze Ahnah gave to her husband that she didn't particularly care for him smoking in the house. The rapid stream of an obvious scolding left Joe looking a bit like a child who'd just gotten caught with his hand in the cookie jar.

Joe gave a sheepish grin and winked at his wife, while Ahnah scowled and carried two bedrolls over by the fire, rolling them out side by side and leaving a stack of folded quilts and pillows on top. She gave Joe another warning look and disappeared back up the stairs.

***

"No man would try to brave this storm," Joe continued after she'd left. "It would be foolish, and if you're still hunting this man then he is not a fool. If he is injured, it would be even more of a risk."

"He'd want to stay hidden," Audrey said.

"Not difficult to do here. There's a mostly abandoned town at the end of the north road. It used to be filled with those searching for gold, but the gold ran out and the people left. There are lots of empty buildings."

"We've been there," Audrey said dryly, thinking of the warehouse and the contraband whales. "We followed his trail as long as we could, but he left the road and it looked as if his tracks continued northwest. The storm was getting worse by that time and we had to turn back. Is there any place in that direction where he could take shelter?"

"Nothing," Joe said, his gray bushy eyebrows raising almost to his hairline. The surprise in his voice made the hair on her arms stand up. "There is nothing but hills and snow. It is not an easy path and there are signs telling all who go in that direction to turn back and go another way. Even in good weather, that path is a death wish."

"Why?" Archer asked.

"Because it's The End of the World. Didn't you research your Alaskan history before you came here?"

"Not well enough, apparently. Why don't you fill us in?"

"It is like the Bermuda Triangle. Only in Alaska. There are places like these all over the world. Where strange phenomena occur that no one can explain. Where a person just vanishes into thin air. Or drops off the face of the planet." He shrugged. "See what I mean? The End of the World. All of those who have set out to find it have never returned. No bodies have ever been recovered. It's as if they ceased to exist the moment they went past the warning signs."

"So you're saying our guy went into the Alaskan Bermuda Triangle?" Archer asked incredulously.

The look on his face was so comical Audrey almost laughed. *Almost*. She had a feeling she'd probably pushed him as far as he'd allow for the day. She had to admit it sounded crazy. Maybe Joe had been smoking his pipe too much.

"It's one of the possibilities," Joe said.

"What's the other?" Audrey asked.

"That he circled back and is hiding in town the same as you are."

CHAPTER NINE

A million tiny men marched through Shane's skull. And he was pretty sure they had nails on the bottom of their shoes.

His eyes inched open, the inside of his eyelids gritty with what felt like sand, and the biting sting of sunlight had him slamming them closed again.

"Shi—" he didn't quite have the strength to get the word out. His throat felt like he'd swallowed shards of glass and chased it with acid.

He did remember enough to know that he was home—in the small cabin he'd built for himself on the MacKenzie Security property. Or the cabin he'd started building. He'd completed the main living area first so he at least had a roof over his head while the rest was being built.

Of all his brothers and his sister, he was the one who needed his space the most. He didn't like falling over siblings and cousins every time he turned around, so when Declan had started building the MacKenzie Security headquarters in Surrender, and he'd offered Shane land to build his own place behind the guarded walls of the compound, he'd jumped at the chance. And he'd insisted on hauling wood and hammering nails while he was on leave.

It wasn't a large place. The main cabin had four walls and a stone fireplace that had been a bitch to build. He'd had to get help from his brother, Grant, to make sure it wouldn't set his house on fire the first time he used it. The work had been hard, but he was damned proud of what he'd created with his own two hands.

The frames for the two bedrooms on each side of the living area were up and ready for someone to finish them. And the kitchen at the back of the house was closed in and ready for finish work. He'd have to hire the rest out. There was no way he'd be able to finish building it on his own. Hell, what was even the point? It wasn't like there was a purpose behind it anymore. He'd be just fine living in the confined corners of the main cabin, his bed shoved into a corner and a loaf of bread, a jar of peanut butter, and plastic utensils on the card table he'd set up in the other corner.

The sun glared through the open blinds and tiny dust motes danced in the brightness. He had no idea what time it was. Or what day for that matter. His hand moved slowly to the side, snagging on the soft sheets of his bed. At least he'd made it to the bed this time. That was a step in the right direction. He would have smiled at the thought if it hadn't hurt so bad to move his muscles.

And true to form, the spot next to him on the bed was empty. No woman wanted to fuck a cripple. He'd probably better get used to that too. No SEAL team to lead and no groupies to fuck.

He groaned and pulled the pillow over his head, hoping to either suffocate himself or at least stop the pounding. But it didn't work. And it turned out the pounding was coming from his front door instead of inside his head. Mostly.

"Goway," he muttered into the pillow. But the knocking turned into pounding. Whoever it was at the door was a persistent bastard. Probably one of his damned brothers or some other well-meaning relative. He was falling over MacKenzies every time he turned around.

"I hope you're decent," a woman yelled from

the other side of the door. "And if you're not, I'm coming in anyway."

Shane looked down the length of his naked body and quickly tossed the sheet over himself. There'd been a time when he'd have called her bluff and let her walk in on him, but there was no way in hell he wanted anyone to look at his body now. Big, strong Shane MacKenzie reduced to nothing but scars that didn't mean shit in the grand scheme of things and no leg. He was no prize, that was for damned sure.

The doorknob rattled, and he breathed out a sigh of relief when he realized it was locked and she'd have to go away. It wasn't like he was going to haul himself to the door. But then a key slipped into the lock and he heard the tumblers turn as loud as cannon fire in his aching head.

The door opened, and Shane was struck speechless as a woman he'd never seen before came inside bold as you please, slamming the door behind her. At least it felt like a slam to his pounding skull.

He grabbed his head in misery and yelled, "What the fuck, lady?"

She only arched a brow and went around to all the windows, opening the blinds so the entire room was cast in blindingly white light. She didn't respond to his outrage. The look on her face was pleasant, but determined. She wore blue scrubs and her dark blonde hair was pulled back in a ponytail. Her face was scrubbed free of makeup. There was nothing remarkable he could see about her on first glance. Her body was small, and it didn't look like she had any curves to speak of. She was just— average.

"Umm—hello? Last time I checked, you needed an invitation before you just barge into someone's home. And in case you haven't noticed, I'm not fit for company."

"Oh, I noticed," she finally said, her task of opening all of the blinds complete. The sun shone at her back, so it was hard for him to see her as she started toward him. "It's time for physical therapy. I'm Doctor Shaw."

"No offense, lady. But there's no way in hell I'm getting out of bed this morning. I had a rough night."

"I have a nose that smells, so believe me, I'm aware of the kind of night you had."

Shane gritted his teeth as his temper began to boil. His brothers always accused him of having a short fuse. It was true for the most part, except when he was on a mission—because temper would

only get his men killed—and around women—
because his mother would have bashed him upside
the head if he'd ever been anything but respectful.
But there was something about this Doctor Shaw
that immediately set his teeth on edge.

"Listen, lady. I don't know who sent you, but
you can go back to the hospital and work with
someone else. I'd prefer to have my old PT doctor
anyway. He's big enough to catch me if I fall."

"I'm stronger than I look," she said, moving a
little closer so the sun at her back wasn't quite as
bright.

Shane almost snorted out a laugh at that
statement. She was so tiny a strong wind could've
blown her away. But right as he had the thought, he
finally got a good look at her face. Average had
been his first thought on seeing her. But he hadn't
gotten a good look at those eyes. He'd never seen
eyes like that before. They weren't blue—they were
a brilliant amethyst. And they changed a rather
ordinary face into a remarkable one.

His body responded in a way it hadn't since
before his accident and he sat up in bed, bunching
the covers over his lap, and swung his foot to the
floor. He leaned his elbows on his knees and
propped his aching head up with his hands as he

tried to get himself under control.

"Sorry, lady, but you'd snap in half like a toothpick. And I'm not exactly in the best mood. I'm just saving you the grief of getting your feelings hurt and crying your way back to the hospital. I'm an asshole. And I have no plans to change. So no offense, but fuck off."

She actually had the audacity to laugh at him, and the anger inside of him boiled a little hotter—a little higher. He lifted his head from his hands so he could stare her down. There weren't many who didn't shrivel under that look from him. His brothers were the only ones he could think of. But she didn't budge. She just matched his glare with one of her own.

"MacKenzie, I was an Army medic for a lot of years. I'm used to assholes. And I could drop you on your ass if I wanted to without batting an eyelash. It'll be a cold day in hell before someone like you has me running away in tears. Now get up and let's get you in the shower so I can actually start breathing through my nose again."

He practically felt the steam coming out of his ears and his pulse pounded in his throat. "You're fired. Don't let the door hit you on the way out."

She leaned closer, so her face was just a few

inches from his own, and those damned eyes were boring into his soul. He hadn't looked past the color. He recognized those eyes. They had the same steely determination as any of the men he commanded or those who'd seen too much in the line of duty.

"You can't fire me. I'm not a doctor at the hospital. I work for MacKenzie Security. So if you want me fired, you're going to have to take it up with your brother. I work for him and no one else."

Fucking figured. His hands fisted against the sheets as he tried to figure out a way to just get her out of there. She was going to be trouble.

"Listen, sweetheart. I'm flattered you're so determined to get me up and moving, but the only thing I'm interested in doing with you is putting you flat on your back and fucking that know-it-all smirk right off your face. You're not exactly my type, but it's not like I'm surrounded by Frog Hogs anymore," he said, referring to the groupies of women who liked sleeping with SEALs. "So I guess I'll make an exception. But I'm telling you, you're better off telling my brother to fuck off and bring in someone else."

There was no change in the expression on her face, just a slight arching of her eyebrow that made his dick twitch.

"I don't fuck spoiled little boys who are feeling sorry for themselves. I fuck men. And they walk away grateful," she said, the corner of her mouth tilting up in a sly smile.

"You mean you don't fuck cripples?" Shane asked, the rage inside him so hot and violent his body shook.

"Mackenzie, if you think a man is made by how many limbs he has, then you're in sorrier shape than I gave you credit for. Now get up."

He fought for control as the battle raged inside of him. She wasn't going to give up. He could see it on her face. But he wasn't going to give up either. He wanted her gone. He wanted to be left alone. And by the time he was finished, she'd be happy to leave him to wallow in his own misery.

CHAPTER TEN

Four days of miserable weather pounded the west coast of Alaska, burying it in layer after layer of snow and ice.

It had taken Audrey less than twenty-four hours for stir-crazy to set in. The days and nights had blurred into one another—the snow and wind a relentless force. The only difference between day and night was the sky going from a stormy gray to pitch black and back again.

She needed to get out and search for Jonah. The back of her neck had been itching ever since the snow had begun to slow. He was out there. And he was close. He had to be.

Joe and Ahnah's tiny house had one bathroom

upstairs with a shower that was so small it was difficult to scrub without knocking elbows against the faucet. But she'd escaped to the small space to put some space between her and Archer, and she let the hot water beat down on her as she tried to think of anything else.

He was driving her crazy, and it hadn't helped that she'd spent each night lying inches away from a man who intrigued her both physically and intellectually.

She'd never met a man like Archer before. He was an unusual mix of being both an open book and secretive as hell. Fascinating was the only word that came to mind. She knew he had a daughter he loved more than anything, and that he'd been divorced for more than a decade. His ex-wife hadn't wanted to live with the secrecy and constant travel, and Archer hadn't blamed her for wanting to move on. They maintained a friendly enough relationship for his daughter's sake, but there'd been no other woman long term in his life.

She knew he liked old black and white movies and he hated Chinese food. She knew his sense of humor edged toward the ridiculous and he could make her laugh at the oddest moments. And she knew he slept flat on his back with his gun tucked just under his sleep mat where he could reach it easily.

Just like she knew in her gut that he'd been the agent known as Warlock during his time with the CIA. But she could never get him to confirm or deny her suspicions. He'd been happy to share whatever she wanted to know about his personal life, but his professional life had been completely off limits.

The stories about Declan's team were legendary. They'd been an unstoppable force and there were contracts out for each of them in multiple countries. She couldn't blame Declan for building his fortress of solitude in bumfuck Montana, surrounded by gated walls and armed guards. Gabe Brennan had basically done the same thing with the operation he'd set up on the other side of the ocean. But Kane Huxley was in hell where he deserved to be, Warlock was rumored to be dead as well, and Cypher was in the wind, living behind his computers and anonymity.

These were men whose pasts would one day catch up with them if they weren't very careful. Not to mention their families being caught in the crossfire.

Being confined in close quarters with Archer was sending her sexually deprived body into overdrive. She hadn't even wanted to look at a man that way since Jonah betrayed her, but Archer had gotten under her skin. A long look from across the table as they played cards or told war stories. A subtle touch against the back of her hand or neck. He was worming his way right inside of her heart, and she didn't know how to stop it.

The problem was she *liked* him. But she didn't trust him. Couldn't allow herself to make that mistake again. But God—she wanted to so badly. It had been too long since she'd felt a man's touch— rough hands sliding over her skin and the smooth glide of bodies joined in heat.

If she'd wanted to forget him, taking a shower might not have been the best idea. The water sprayed hot and forceful over naked flesh to the point where Audrey was almost too stimulated. Her hands skimmed over her shoulders and down her arms, and her eyes closed as she imagined it was Archer's touch instead of her own.

Her moan was drowned out by the spray of the water as she cupped her breasts, heavy with need, her nipples beaded into small peaks of pure sensation. Her thumbs skimmed across each one and she felt the pull in the swollen flesh between her thighs.

Her hands continued down, over the scars

across her ribs and stomach where she no longer had any feeling at all, to the soft black curls that covered her sex. With her eyes closed, it was easy to imagine Archer kneeling before her and his fingers teasing the moist folds of her pussy.

Inhibition disappeared and her head dropped back to her shoulders. A moan, this one louder than the last, took her by surprise as feelings she hadn't experienced in years sent shivers coursing through her body. She was hungry—needy—for that physical touch. And not just any man's touch. She wasn't ready for that. But she was ready for Archer, and the slick syrup coating her fingers told her he would be the one to bring her body back to life.

Audrey's fingertip barely skimmed across the taut nub of her clit, and chills broke out across her skin as she continued the whispered caress. She sucked in a shuddering, broken breath as sensation shot through her, tightening the muscles in her stomach and making the ones in her thighs tremble.

It was good. For three years her body had starved while her mind and soul healed, and she hadn't even been able to touch herself as she was doing now. It had taken meeting Archer to wake her again. But the fingers rubbing slow circles across her clit weren't the same as having him there with her. She needed the feel of him hot and hard, pushing between the plump folds of her pussy and making her scream in pleasure.

Her fingers moved faster, across the dewy folds as her juices combined with the water, and her breathing became erratic and her moans more frantic as she came closer to orgasm.

She expected it to hit her with the force of a tidal wave. Desire had been dormant for three long years, and she braced her other hand against the shower wall as she felt the warning tingles gather inside her. But when the orgasm hit, it wasn't with the breathtaking force she'd been expecting. It was a gentle roll through her body—enough to take the edge off but not enough to satisfy completely.

Her breath came in rough pants and she squeezed her eyes closed in disappointment. Maybe she wasn't as ready as she wanted to be. Or maybe she was just out of practice. Whatever the case, she turned off the water with an annoyed flick of her wrist and grabbed a towel, drying herself off quickly.

She dressed in the clothes Ahnah had washed, and she brushed out her hair, braiding it quickly so it was out of her face. She used the toothbrush that had been given to her and made sure she'd left everything as she'd found it before making her escape. She was more annoyed with herself than anything for thinking she could force her body to do things it wasn't ready for. Maybe Jonah had ruined her chances of having complete satisfaction ever again.

Audrey opened the door and stopped short when she saw Archer standing only a few feet away, a folded towel and change of clothes in his hands.

"Did you have a good shower?" he asked.

She felt heat flood her cheeks and hoped he couldn't see her blush. He moved a step closer and her body responded as if she hadn't just orgasmed only minutes before. She realized her mistake even as she fought to keep from taking a step back and putting more distance between them. She'd only taken the edge off of her need, and the want for him was as strong as ever. But the thought of making herself that vulnerable to another man again had her throat closing in fear. She wasn't sure her needs and common sense were ever going to come to terms.

"You okay?"

"I'm fine. Just ready to get out of here."

"Joe says we'll have clear skies in the next couple of hours and the weather will stay that way for the next few days."

"Did he see that in his pipe smoke?"

"Nah, he was listening to the weather on the short wave radio." The corner of Archer's mouth turned up in a half smile. He had a nice smile. It was one of the first things she'd noticed about him. "You're looking a little flushed, Sharpe. You sure you're okay?"

"Never been better," she lied.

"Then if you don't mind," he said, arching a brow and nodding his head toward the bathroom door. "I think it's my turn now."

The heat in his gaze left no doubt that he'd guessed what she'd been doing in the shower, and it left no doubt what he'd be doing either. She felt the flame in her cheeks rise hotter and she stepped aside so he could get by. Before she could escape down the stairs he stopped her.

"You can trust me, you know," he said. "You may not believe me, but I'd never do anything to hurt you. Maybe at some point we can figure out a way to help convince you of that."

She didn't turn back to face him. Her pulse was already beating wildly in her throat at the possibility of what he was suggesting. She wasn't so dead that she didn't recognize male interest when she saw it.

SIZZLE

Audrey escaped while she still had the chance and headed downstairs.

***

Two hours later, the sky cleared just as the weatherman had predicted and the sun glared off the mounds of snow blanketing the area.

It turned out Joe had all of the supplies they needed for their journey. Through the back door of his small house was another building twice the size filled with everything an outdoorsman could possibly want. Apparently, Joe owned the only outdoor supply store along the entire west coast of Alaska. Good business for Joe, and extremely fortuitous for them.

They'd been outfitted in extra winter gear—thermal suits that fit tight against the skin, lined ski pants, a pullover that was too warm unless you were outside in the cold, and down jackets with fur-lined hoods. Water and individually wrapped containers of trail mix and jerky went into their packs along with a First Aid Kit.

Joe rolled a tent, bedrolls, and a few other provisions into two bundles for each of them to carry on their backs. They weren't traveling light, but with the outdoor conditions the way they were they needed to take every precaution for their survival. The Alaskan wilderness was nothing to toy with.

Joe also had an entire arsenal at the back of his shop for hunters, and she picked up a couple of Glock 9mm's—her favorite—and a shoulder holster that fit fairly well beneath the down jacket. She picked up an extra knife for the inside of her boot and noticed Archer's weapons choices were similar to her own. More than likely, any contact they had with Salt would be close contact. They needed him alive so they could get the detonation codes from him.

"I've got something special, just for the two of you," Joe said as he went behind the counter to the locked gun case. "It's a surprise."

"I hate surprises," Audrey murmured under her breath, making Archer cough to cover his laugh.

Joe pulled open a drawer and Archer let out a long low whistle. "I'm not even going to ask how you're in possession of these kinds of weapons."

Joe just grinned and waved a hand, unconcerned. "You want?" he said, waggling his eyebrows.

"I definitely want," Audrey said, reaching for the submachine gun. It had three different settings, so she could shoot one bullet at a time or the whole magazine if she so desired. She hooked it across the bulging pack on her back for easier transport while Archer did the same.

"You ready?" he asked, making a final adjustment of his weapons so he could reach them all easily.

"Yeah. Question is, how are we going to get where we're going?"

"I can help you with that," Joe said. "You know how to ride the sled dogs, yes?"

"No—" She and Archer both said in unison.

"It's either the dogs or cross country skis. Snowmobiles will run out of fuel before you make it to The End of the World," Joe shrugged. "There is no other way to travel. There are three roads that lead out of Nome, but each of them leads to nowhere. They are literally called The Roads to Nowhere. We are very funny here in Alaska."

Audrey pressed her lips together to keep from smiling. She could practically feel Archer's frustration.

"The land is treacherous. So if you want to get where you're going in a hurry, you take the dogs."

Audrey shared a look with Archer and she raised her brows, telling him without speaking that the choice was up to him. It didn't seem like they had any other option, and she saw by the resigned look on his face that he realized that as well.

"I guess we're taking the dogs."

CHAPTER ELEVEN

Joe had been right. The dogs were a much faster mode of transportation for covering such a large expanse of land. They were also smart and trained well enough to ignore their inexperienced riders. They'd unloaded all of their supplies, except for the guns, into the cargo basket.

It was an eight-dog team, and the moment Audrey stepped onto the sled and held onto the driving bar she saw the problem. But it was too late to voice a protest when Archer stepped up behind her, his large body surrounding hers as his hands gripped the handle bars.

The claustrophobia took her completely by surprise. She'd never suffered from it before, but she'd also never been all but swallowed whole by a man like Archer. Her skin turned hot and clammy beneath the layers of her clothes and black spots wavered in front of her eyes.

"Just take a deep breath," he said, his voice soft enough that Joe and Ahnah couldn't hear as they watched to wave them off. "My hands will stay right here." He flexed them around the bar deliberately. "You're in control of the team."

She did as he said and took in a deep breath, the cold stinging her lungs and then coming out in white puffs. Her head cleared and she got control of herself. "I'm fine. I'm ready."

She followed the instructions Joe had given her for starting up the team and they took off like a shot across the snow, pointed in the direction of what Joe called The End of the World.

"Oh, man. My daughter would love this," Archer said into her ear. "I'm going to have to take her to do this on our next vacation."

Audrey realized she had a big grin on her face as the snow slushed up around them, the speed of the dogs exhilarating. The sun seemed twice as bright as normal against the white of the landscape, and not even the protective shades she wore could cut the glare completely.

"You do a lot of stuff like this with her?" she asked, settling into the rhythm of the moving sled, adjusting her weight as needed.

"We don't get a lot of time together, so I always make sure we do something memorable. She's a bit of a daredevil and she likes adventures, so it's not always easy finding something that's not completely crazy and still safe for a sixteen-year-old."

"She sounds a lot like you."

"Yeah. It drives her mother crazy."

Audrey heard the smile in his voice and turned her head to look up at him, returning the smile. But it faded as she saw how close his face was to her own. She felt the warmth of his breath against her lips. but didn't dare give into the temptation to glance down and look at them. Instead, her gaze was caught in his dark stare.

It was one of those moments where time seemed to stop as the world continued to rush by around them. She somehow found the strength to turn away, but it had taken more resolve than she'd expected, and she'd had to take a moment to get her racing heart under control.

Archer kept his word and didn't move his

hands from the bar, but she couldn't help but notice how the front of his body was pressed against hers. Every jostle and turn had their bodies pressing closer until sweat gathered beneath the layers of her clothes and her body was responding in ways that had nothing to do with the hunt.

What the hell was wrong with her? Nothing had ever come between her and the job before. Not even Jonah. She'd been able to compartmentalize her feelings for him while they were on a mission. But Archer was wreaking havoc with her concentration.

She couldn't seem to control the response of her body. It was chemical—plain and simple. Every mile they traveled became more unbearable. Her breasts grew heavy and her breathing changed, her pulse thudding wildly beneath her skin. It took every ounce of control she had not to press back against him and see if he was as hard and ready for her as she was wet for him.

Fortunately, the dogs helped solve the problem. About halfway to their destination, just past the sign Joe had told them about warning trespassers to turn back or risk death, the dogs pulled up sharp, and if she hadn't had a good grip on the drive bar she would've dumped them both onto the ground. She pressed her foot to the brake, and she had to fight to keep the sled upright, so Archer lent his strength to hold them steady while she called out commands to the dogs.

The sudden silence was unnerving and she slowly released the white knuckled grip she had on the bar.

"What the hell?" she breathed out in a rush, though she didn't expect an answer.

The dogs moved restlessly, some of them whimpering as they lay down in the snow, letting her know with certainty that they had no plans to continue on.

She and Archer got off the sled, each of them reaching for the weapons beneath their jackets. They were in the middle of open land in all directions. There were no trees for cover. Just rolling hills of snow. But something had spooked the dogs. Joe had told them they were very intuitive and to pay attention.

They moved into a position where they stood back to back, their weapons up and ready for attack if it came. All they could do was listen. But the question was *what* had spooked the dogs? As far as she could tell, there was nothing to make them react as they had.

Silence lay heavy like a blanket with only the occasional rattle of the harness breaking through. There were no fresh tracks in the snow. Nothing but the two of them and wide open land.

"You want to walk out a little ways?" Archer suggested. "We can circle around, see if we can find what's got the dogs riled."

"Maybe they're not fans of The End of the World," she said, dryly. "Though by my calculations we still have more than a hundred miles to go before we get there."

"At least. Even with the snowmobile, Salt would've been cutting it close outracing the storm, considering how quickly it moved in."

"He would've planned for all contingencies. He might have arrived in Alaska a day ahead of me, but I promise you he's been here before. He knows the land. Knows the area. He's a paranoid son of a bitch."

She did as Archer suggested and moved ahead of the dogs, going clockwise to Archer's counterclockwise until they'd eventually meet in the middle.

Neither of them had elected to wear snowshoes so they could move quickly if they needed to—they weren't great for maneuverability and she'd rather take her chances on her own two feet. The downside was the snow came up above her knees, and in some places up to her thighs and hips, as she trudged through.

It turned out the slow movement and depth of the snow was a blessing in disguise. The sound of the trigger as her foot came down was no louder than a click. But it was a sound she'd heard before.

"Oh, shit," she said, but the words came out as a strangled whisper. Her muscles froze and the cold sweat of fear raced down her back.

The good news was the land mine didn't automatically detonate as soon as she'd pressed the trigger. But if she took her foot off the mechanism, they'd be finding little pieces of her body in the snow for months.

"Archer," she said as calmly as she could. She held herself steady, one foot keeping the trigger of the land mine pressed down.

He must have recognized the urgency in her voice because he put his gun back in the holster and shuffled in her direction, his feet scooting through the snow instead of taking steps so he didn't end up in the same predicament.

She had to give him credit, he didn't even consider leaving her there to fend for herself and saving his own ass. He came right to her, despite not knowing how dangerous the situation, and his ass was on the line right next to hers.

"I guess we know what the dogs don't like about the area," he said, looking her in the eye with a calm assurance that had her shoulders relaxing a bit. He wasn't going to leave her.

"Let me get a look at what we've got, and then we'll figure out what to do about it. Don't go anywhere."

She choked out a nervous laugh as he knelt by her feet and dug down into the snow, carefully tunneling around the mine.

"There she is," he said.

"So there's gender assigned to land mines?" She stared straight ahead, her gaze locking in on a crag of snow covered rocks about twenty yards away. Her hands fisted at her sides and she just focused on breathing in and out—for as long as she could.

"I figure anything designed to blow up and hurl shrapnel should be called she. I've been married before, so I remember. I've got a nice scar behind one ear from a perfume bottle that was thrown at my head."

"At least she didn't shoot you."

She felt him pause, so she glanced down to find humor filled eyes looking back at her. "Did you just make a joke? I think there's hope for you yet, Agent Sharpe."

"Not if we're both blown to bits while you're taking your sweet time down there. Leave it to a man to make things as complicated as possible."

"It's not me standing on a land mine now, is it?"

Audrey couldn't argue with that logic so she just grunted and watched him go back to work. He lay down on his stomach so his head touched the snow and looked at it from the side. He moved back to his knees and glanced up at her.

"Looks pretty standard as far as land mines go. I'm going to borrow the knife in your boot. Don't let it freak you out when I touch you."

She nodded and his hand slipped inside her boot where she'd put her knife. He bent back to the mine and she heard the tiny scrapes as he worked the tip of the knife at the mechanism.

"I just realized it's been a while since I knelt at a woman's feet. And usually she's naked while I'm doing it and not standing on an explosive device. We should try it that way next time."

She choked out another laugh and stared down at the top of his head. His voice didn't betray any of the urgency he must have felt. Mines like the one she was standing on could go off at a moment's notice. And though his voice was level, she saw the sweat beaded on his skin as he continued to work.

Audrey felt the knife slide back into her boot and he came to his feet, his body only inches from hers.

"Pick up your foot."

She stared at him for a long moment, knowing she had to trust that he'd taken care of things or they would both end up dead. And then she took a deep breath and prayed.

"Wait a minute—"

Audrey froze, her heart pounding as he issued the order, terror coursing through her veins as she waited for the explosion to hit. And then her eyes widened as he leaned in and took her mouth in a kiss that rocked her straight to her soul. Her entire universe exploded into a million pieces.

She hadn't prepared herself for the possibility of his taste—not yet—not when she hadn't guarded herself against the feelings she'd started to develop for him. His tongue slipped past her lips and she heard a moan in the distance—it must have been hers—but the blood rushing in her ears muted her senses so the only thing she was aware of was the man possessing her like he had every right to. It was terrifying. It was exhilarating. And she realized in that moment that every lover she'd ever had, never touched her the way Archer was doing now.

It was just a kiss. But there was nothing simple about it. She felt stripped bare, as if he were already buried as far inside her as he could possibly be. He invaded her mind, body, and soul, and she was helpless to resist him.

Tremors shook her body and her hands came up and gripped his shoulders, holding on as her equilibrium tilted. The heat of him drew her to him like a moth to flame, and his hands roamed down her body and gripped her hips, jerking her up against him so she could feel the hardness of his cock through the layers of clothing he wore. She arched against him, aching for the kind of release she'd needed in the shower that morning.

It was then she realized both of her feet were suspended in the air, and the mine lay disabled on the ground. She pulled back, her breath coming in short pants and her eyes wide with the shock of whatever had just happened.

"Why'd you do that?" she whispered, though she didn't think to let go of his shoulders, and he didn't set her feet on the ground.

"I figured if we were going to die we might as well enjoy ourselves on the way out." His breath was just as erratic as hers, and she felt the heat of his fingers through the layers of clothes.

"This is a bad idea, Archer." She pushed against his chest until he sat her back on her feet and then released her. It annoyed her that her legs were just a little unsteady—more so because of the kiss than the threat of the land mine, which was saying something about its potency.

His lips twitched with his normal good humor, but his eyes remained serious. "You have to admit, it was a good kiss. Being naked while doing it would probably be somewhere on the scale of spectacular."

"The last time I was naked with a man, I ended up with three bullets in the chest. You can understand my hesitancy."

"It's a quandary. I'm trying to figure out a way

around that so you're not so skittish. I'll let you know when I come up with something."

"Unbelievable," she said, shaking her head, though she had to laugh at his audacity. "You have a skull harder than rock."

"Believe it or not, I've been told that before. You see this scar here," he said, running his fingers along the side of his scalp. "It's from a bullet. Went right in and bounced off my skull. You and me, Sharpe. We live charmed lives."

"The thing about that is the charm eventually runs out and you die."

"Which is why we should take life's pleasures where we find them. I've got a little place down in Costa Rica. We should go when this is done. You can wear your bikini."

"Yes, and horrify all the tourists with my scars. I'll pass. Maybe we could worry about finding Salt before you start making vacation plans."

He gave her a curious look and took hold of her arm before she could walk away. "He's *Proteus* isn't he? Salt? I don't know why I didn't put it together before now. But it's the only thing that makes sense."

She'd known it wasn't a secret she'd be able to

keep forever, and she would've told him. Eventually. When she'd known for sure that she could trust him with that kind of classified information.

"He needs to die," she said instead. "How many agents lost their lives because of him? How many innocent people?"

"You don't have to convince me that he needs to die. But it would've been nice information to have going in all the same."

"Now you know. And our goal is still the same." She moved around him and headed back toward the sled.

"I don't suppose there are any other pertinent facts you need to pass on," he called out. "Now's as good of a time as any."

"You talk in your sleep," she shouted back.

He narrowed his eyes and followed after her, and she turned around before he could see her grin. She wondered how long it would take before he asked her what he'd said, but he remained stubbornly silent.

"We're going to have to go around," he eventually said. "Salt wouldn't have booby trapped the entire perimeter. It's too much land to cover."

"You realize if we keep going, we'll be walking right into his trap. There's no place for cover around here. He's going to be waiting for us now—watching."

"Joe marked a spot on the map where another deserted gold mine is located, but it's at least another fifty miles. It'll be dark before we get there, and there's no snow in the forecast to cover our tracks. It'll protect us from walking into Salt's trap, but it'll leave us wide open for the Russians."

The Russians had been worrying her too. "It's a chance we're going to have to take. We're the Russian's primary targets. Not Jonah. They see us as the bigger threat, because if we don't handle this right he could end up detonating every one of those tankers, and that's the last thing they want.

"They'll be out for blood. Ours. And they'll want to make sure we haven't talked. If word gets out that Russian oil tankers are wired with explosives then the trade routes to every country they do business with will be shut down."

"The Russians we can handle. I'm not so sure about Salt. I didn't know what we were getting into when we first started this, but *Proteus* isn't an amateur. He's survived in the darkest parts of underground terrorist organizations for years. We could use some help. MacKenzie Security has a lot of resources. We need to utilize them. There's no reason for you to think you have to take him out alone other than supreme stubbornness on your part."

"Are you trying to piss me off?"

"Probably. How am I doing?"

"You're getting close. And I'm not being stubborn. No one knows Salt and his movements better than I do. He trained me. I'm the best bet we have to find him."

"No one is disputing that. But we've found him. He's at The End of the fucking World. Now we just need to kill him. And for that, you're going to need help. How am I doing now?"

"You've succeeded." She crossed her arms over her chest and arched a brow. "Can we go now or are you going to launch into another diatribe?"

"One day you and I will have a normal conversation."

"I doubt it."

"Maybe over breakfast," he said ignoring her. "You seem like the kind of person who'd enjoy breakfast conversation."

"I'm going to strangle you in your sleep."

"Strangely enough, you haven't been the first person to tell me that either."

Archer checked the compass on his watch and the dogs stood and shook, as if they sensed that he was ready to go.

"I want to find out more about this End of the World and the people who went missing. Maybe Declan has some information. And if not, maybe he has an idea of how we can locate Salt and get past his defenses. Because you're right. He'll be ready for us if we go for him now."

Archer got out the bag of dog treats and gave them to the animals, petting one of the lead dogs behind the ears before he came back to the sled.

"You ready to go?" he asked.

The thought of riding for fifty more miles with her body pressed against him after that kiss sounded like torture, and from his cocky smile, it looked like he knew exactly how torturous it would be.

"Why don't you take the drive bar this time and I'll ride behind you?"

The smile disappeared from his face and he looked down at her lips before shaking his head and getting onto the sled.

"It's probably for the best," he said soberly. "You've got a very bitable neck. I probably wouldn't be able to restrain myself. I'll even let you hold onto me instead of the handle bar if you're nice."

Audrey snorted out a laugh and stepped up behind him. "You're a generous soul, Archer. But you're going to regret making the offer." She wrapped her arms around his waist and pressed her body to his back. He sucked in a deep breath and groaned at the touch.

"Maybe I will," he said in a strained voice. "But I've got you right where I want you. I told you I had some ideas on how to get you to trust me. Though you'd think saving your pretty ass from getting blown into a million pieces would be enough."

"Just mush, Agent Ryan. You make my head spin."

"Well, then. Mission accomplished."

CHAPTER TWELVE

Full darkness had fallen by the time they reached the wooden skeleton of the first building of Devil's Mining Camp. At least that's what Joe had called it. There wasn't any reference to the ghost town on the map other than where he'd circled it in bright red marker.

They'd had to take several breaks along the way for the dogs to rest and eat. And when dusk had settled in, they'd had to stop again to strap on headlamps so they could see where they were going. It had been a long and grueling process, and it would be easy for exhaustion to set in, but they had a long journey still in front of them.

Archer put his foot on the brake and stopped the sled. "This would be a great place for an ambush."

Audrey shivered involuntarily. The town was perfectly preserved under a layer of white, just as it must have looked a hundred years before. It wouldn't have surprised her at all to see the ghosts of men seeking their fortune walking along the narrow street or saloon girls hanging from the windows, beckoning them to come inside out of the cold and get warm for a price.

She unzipped her jacket and pulled her gun out, holding it down by her thigh. The temperatures had dropped drastically after the sun went down and she flexed her grip around the butt, getting the blood flowing through her hands.

"It's creepy," she whispered. She didn't know *why* she was whispering. Only that it seemed like the appropriate thing to do.

"There's no tracks going in that I can see," Archer said, shining the LED light back and forth across the ground. "If anyone's been here, it's been a while. We're going to have to take our chances that Salt didn't plan this far out. The dogs need shelter and rest for the night and so do we."

"Shelter might be overreaching a bit," Audrey said as he got the dogs going again. "We'll be lucky if it doesn't come down on top of us."

"It's lasted this long. I figure it can hold another night."

The town began and ended almost faster than a person could blink. It was just one strip of broken down buildings and nothing else. The structures on the ends were in the worst shape and provided the least amount of protection, so they opted for one of the buildings in the middle. It would at least provide protection from the wind and adequate coverage if anyone tried to sneak up on them.

"I'll take care of the dogs and get them set up if you want to make base camp," he told her. "I need to get on the sat phone and get in touch with Declan. Or maybe you should do that." The look on his face was a little sheepish, and if she wasn't mistaken his cheeks were turning red. "The last time I called he was—busy."

"Whatever that means. I'll call him if you're scared of your boss."

"He's your boss too now. And I don't need any more ideas popping into my head. The night's going to be long enough as it is."

"I have no idea what you're talking about."

"I know you don't." He opened his mouth as if he were going to say something else, but instead breathed out a white puff of air and left her alone in front of what used to be a saloon.

Confused, she decided to ignore him and hefted his pack of supplies over her shoulder along with her own. She imagined the saloon at one time had swinging doors, but they'd long since fallen down, so only black iron hinges were left hanging from the doorframe. She carefully stepped over the threshold, setting her light on wide beam and shining it slowly across the room.

It was a good sized area and seemed sturdy enough. It had wood floors once upon a time, but most of it had rotted, so only the black dirt beneath showed. The rubble of what had probably once been a bar and chairs and tables were scattered throughout, and the staircase that led to the second floor was completely gone, leaving only a gaping hole where it had pulled away from the wall and collapsed in a pile on the ground.

Part of the roof on one side had caved in, so snow had mounded on top of the debris. But she'd camped in worse places, and at least the other half of the room was dry and blocked from the wind.

She dumped both packs in the corner and immediately started taking out their weapons so they were ready in case they needed them in a hurry. She found a warped piece of wood that was still fairly sturdy and lined guns and knives up in a straight line along with extra magazines.

Provisions, maps, and the sat phone came out next, and she found a larger piece of wood so she could lay the map out flat. She almost didn't set up the tent, but it was insolated and the added protection against the cold would make them less miserable. She wasn't sure being confined in such close quarters with Archer was the best of ideas, not after the way his kiss had affected her. She wanted him. And it terrified her.

Audrey looked over at the small arsenal of weapons and grabbed the baby Glock, slipping it into the pocket of her jacket. Just having it close by made her relax a little. Her gut told her Archer Ryan was a man she could trust. He'd proven himself by standing next to her while disarming the land mine. But she was afraid there would always be a part of her from now on that held herself back—waiting and watching—to see if he'd betray her. Wanting the physical release he could give her was one thing. Hoping for anything more than that was a whole other problem.

Before she could talk herself out of it she erected the tent and used what materials she could to stuff around the inside perimeter for insolation. Then she laid out the bedrolls, leaving an adequate amount of space between the two. She finished it off by setting one of the flashlights up in the corner so they wouldn't hurt themselves if they needed to get out quickly. The light only gave it a homey, romantic glow, and she debated turning it off but knew that would be foolish.

"There," she said, nodding, as if trying to convince herself she was on a normal op with a normal partner.

"Are you talking to yourself?" Archer said from behind her.

She didn't jump, but it was damned close. He moved like a wraith. With an unnerving silence for a man of his size and strength.

"We're set up here. I'm going to take a walk around the perimeter while you talk to Declan."

"Coward."

She narrowed her eyes at him, but he just gave her that insufferable grin. "Last time I checked I haven't actually received a paycheck from MacKenzie Security. And to be honest, I'm not all that certain it's where I belong. So until I make that decision, you're the one who can talk to Declan. I never asked for any help on this job. You're the one who elbowed your way in."

He took a step closer and she had to look up to keep eye contact, but she held her ground.

"I would have come for you because that's what my orders were," he said, his smile fading. "But I took one look at your picture and I would've come even if my orders had been to stay as far away from you as possible."

She sneered and her words sounded robotic to her ears. "Just like a man to fall in lust with a face and not think past his hard-on to see if there's anything beneath it. They must have taken out the other pictures from my file. Believe me, my face is the only thing left of beauty on my entire body, and there's nothing left on the inside except the need for revenge."

Anger flashed in his eyes, but his voice was barely a whisper. "That's where you're wrong. And you don't give either of us enough credit. I recognized you the second I saw your picture. How does that settle with that logical brain of yours?"

"I'd say you're living in a fantasy land if you believe in any of that crap."

"What, you don't believe there are unexplainable connections between people? You've never walked down the street or seen someone in passing and felt you've met them before? And be careful before you decide to lie straight to my face."

Audrey pressed her lips tight together to keep from doing just that. She knew exactly the feeling he was speaking of. She'd felt it the first moment their eyes had connected in that warehouse several days before.

He nodded as if she'd made the right decision to keep quiet. "And you're wrong, you know. I did see the other pictures. You made a comment earlier when I asked you to come to Costa Rica with me about scaring the tourists with your scars. Do you know what I saw when I looked at those pictures of what the Syrians had done to you?"

He waited for her answer and she finally managed to get a word past her dry throat. "No."

"I saw unimaginable strength. That's it," he said, taking a step back and giving her a little more room to breathe. "I felt sorrow and anger for what had been done to you, but they're just scars, Audrey. Nothing more. And if you think for a second that I wouldn't stand proudly on a beach anywhere with you in a bikini, then you haven't learned anything about me or the kind of man I am at all these last few days."

Her throat tightened and she felt the burn behind her eyes, but like always, the tears refused to fall. She thanked God for that.

"Go do your perimeter check," he sat, reaching past her to grab the sat phone off the makeshift table she'd made. "I'll call Dec and fill him in."

She nodded and made her escape, feeling like she'd just been given a reprieve.

CHAPTER THIRTEEN

Archer blew out a slow breath as Audrey left him alone. He'd pushed too hard, too fast. The look on her face had confirmed that. All he could do was give her time, and maybe some day she'd realize she could trust him with not only her life—but with her heart.

He couldn't go so far as to say what they had between them was more than a chemical and physical connection for the moment, but he wasn't opposed to exploring to see if it could become something more. And that wasn't something he'd ever thought he'd be willing to try again. He'd given up the thought of having a long-term relationship. But with Audrey, he wanted to try. Because just being next to her, just talking to her—and then God, that kiss—made his body ache and want more than he ever had before.

He was thirty-six years old and was experienced when it came to women. He knew the feelings between him and Audrey were rare, and he wasn't willing to let them go so easily.

Before he could dwell on it anymore, he picked up the satellite phone and called Declan.

"MacKenzie," Dec answered.

"You've sent me into a complete clusterfuck."

"Jesus, Ryan. I just sent you to retrieve one agent. How hard is could it be?"

"Almost fucking impossible when it turns out Jonah Salt is alive and she's been hunting him down like a dog for shooting her three times in the chest. Not only that, but Salt has his foot on Russia's balls by wiring up a few of their oil tankers with explosives and blackmailing them for money. And, oh yeah, did I mention that Jonah Salt is fucking *Proteus*?"

"Fuck me," Dec said, the surprise evident. "Start over from the beginning."

Archer ran through everything that had happened since he'd found Audrey in the warehouse, standing over the bodies of Russian

Intelligence agents.

"What do you need?" Dec finally asked.

"I need as much information as you can get on an area called The End of the World here in Alaska. Your pal Joe told us that it's an area where people go missing. I think that's where Salt is hiding. And I need Cypher on the tech end of this. I don't want to stumble across any more land mines or something worse. I want satellite imaging and heat seeking capability."

"Hold on a sec," Declan said. "Cal is here in the office. I'm putting him on speaker."

Cal Colter, also known as Cypher in the hacking community, could work magic with any technology and could build something out of nothing. He was like MacGyver on steroids.

"This is what happens when you send a woman in to do a man's job," Cal said through the speaker. "Hope you took plenty of tampons with you."

"Fuck you, Cyph." He heard laughter on the other end of the line and rolled his eyes. "And you're damned lucky the new recruit isn't in here right now. She'd cut off your balls with the big ass knife she carries in her boot."

"Ooh, that sounds pretty hot. Let me guess,

she's about six-feet tall and can piss while she's standing up. I bet she has a chest hairier than yours. Dec sure knows how to pick 'em."

"Because I always hire agents based on what they look like instead of skill," Dec said dryly. "Don't be an ass, Cal."

"Hey, I'm just calling it like I see it. They'd rather look and act like men rather than use their feminine skills to bring down the bad guys."

"There's a woman out there somewhere who's going to bring you down a peg one day," Dec told him. "I hope I get to shake her hand."

Archer laughed. "Are you kidding me? Are you talking about him having an actual long-term relationship with a flesh and blood woman? Not One Night Cal," he said, referring to the nickname an old fling had given him. "Besides, Miranda might get jealous."

Cal's pride and joy was a computer he'd built and designed for MacKenzie Security. He'd named her Miranda and she had a voice like a sex kitten. No one could touch Miranda except for Cal. And their relationship just wasn't natural.

"Miranda is going to save your sorry ass," Cal said, offended. "You'd better be nice to her."

"You realize she's not a real person, right?" Archer asked.

"Sure she is," Cal said. "She's the perfect woman. She does everything I tell her to do and never argues."

Archer heard the click of a keyboard over the line. Cal was never still or quiet while he worked his magic. The thing about working with the same people for a lot of years and in high pressure situations was that you got to know them better than your own family. You learned their strengths and weaknesses, the things that set them off or the triggers that could paralyze them at the worst of times.

Just like he knew Cal's attitude toward women was a complete façade to protect himself. He'd lost his wife and both parents in an attack shortly after he'd joined the CIA, and he still blamed himself for not thinking to bury their identities better than just on a cursory level. Cypher had been born not long after that.

Audrey came back inside their makeshift campground and he watched her as she dug through her pack for a couple of power bars. She tossed him one and he caught it easily, as well as the bottle of water that followed.

Her face was scrubbed clean and he figured she'd given herself a face full of snow just like he had to wake herself up. The extreme cold was dangerous because it could make a person lethargic, and after the adrenaline rush they'd had when she'd stepped on that land mine, they were both running on fumes.

"That's interesting," Cal said.

"Interesting good or interesting bad?" Archer asked.

"Probably bad. It's going to take some time before I can get you the satellite imaging and heat signals. Someone's trying to fuck with Miranda. Whatever is at The End of the World, someone doesn't want us to find out about it. My screen is going crazy, but Miranda's got it under control. We'll just reverse the virus and see where that leaves us, right baby?"

"I'll assume he's talking to the computer," Archer said.

"I fully expect to come in the office one day and find a note telling me he's eloped to Tahiti with his computer," Dec said. "The boy isn't right. Speaking of tropical paradises, how many days of provisions do you have?"

"About a week's worth."

"Keep the phone close by and give us some time to work it from this end. Stay put for now."

Archer heard the click in his ear and tossed the phone back on the makeshift table. "Looks like this is our new home for a little while. At least until Cal can get us a satellite image so we can keep going. Miranda has this program that can show anything with a pulse in a 3d image as if it were standing right in front of you. It's pretty cool."

"Miranda?"

"Oh, Cal's computer. She's amazing. But don't tell Cal I said so. His head's big enough. She'll also be able to do a search and scan for any more land mines or other devices he might have set."

"Handy. If she can do all that, I won't even make fun of him for naming an inanimate object when I finally meet him."

She put the trash in a sealed bag and then looked around their living space before finally zeroing in on him. Archer wondered if she'd get around to looking him in the eye again. He wasn't sure what her feelings toward him would be after their earlier conversation.

"I've decided to have sex with you," she said

after a few seconds.

He'd chosen that unfortunate moment to take a drink, and he choked on the water, wheezing as it went down wrong. His eyes watered as he tried to suck in a breath and he pounded on his chest while she watched him with an arched brow and a patient look on her face.

"I'm sorry, what did you say?"

She bent down and started unlacing her boots, and he watched in fascination as she removed a small arsenal from the space. "You don't have to look so shocked. It's not like I'm asking you to commit treason. It's just sex."

"Umm—"

"Besides, the friction and shared body heat will keep us warm."

"Now wait a min—" his mouth went dry as she untied the drawstring on her insulated pants. Who knew a gesture like that could be so sexy? He scrubbed his hands over his face and tried to keep his blood in his brain instead of pooling into his lap.

"Wait—" He took hold of her hands before she could disrobe any further. "That's all this would be to you?" he asked, surprised at the hurt he felt. She was offering any man's dream. "You all of a sudden are ready for sex after all this time and I'm just supposed to lay down and let you have your way with me?"

"Do you have a problem with that?"

"A little, yeah."

"I don't play games, Archer. Not outside of my professional life. Time is too short to try and figure out what other people are feeling and thinking. So I'll tell you straight out. I haven't wanted another man since Jonah. Haven't even been able to think of a man in that way since then. But I want you. What else do you want from me?"

"Your trust," he said immediately. "I want to know that you'll take me inside you and feel all of me. That your mind will be focused solely on how good I can make you feel. Not on whether or not I'm going to stick a knife in your back or hurt you in some other way."

"You want me to trust you, but what do I really know about you? I've got good instincts, but they've been wrong before. I've got the word of Declan MacKenzie—a man I respect and am a little in awe of. And I've got the man you want me to see. The one who cracks jokes at the wrong time and who watches me with patient and calculating eyes, while undressing me at the same time."

"Sweetheart, I'm an open book. What you see is what you get."

He could practically see her teeth grinding together. "Don't call me sweetheart," she gritted out. "And if you're such an open book then I should be able to ask you anything I want and get an honest answer."

"One—" he said. "One question only. And then it's my turn."

She hesitated at that, but finally nodded.

"What do you want to know?"

"Are you Warlock?"

"Warlock's dead. And dead men don't walk among the living." She sneered at him and he had the sudden urge to bite her plump bottom lip. His cock went rock hard at the thought.

"An open book, huh? And you wonder why I don't trust you."

"That's the problem. You *do* trust me. You're just too much of a coward to acknowledge it."

"That's the second time you've called me a coward. It better be the last."

"Or what? You're finally going to put your

money where your mouth is?" He took a step closer until the tips of his boots touched her toes. "Here's my question for you. Do you think you'll be satisfied with the quick fuck you're asking for? Or will you keep coming back for more?" He watched the pulse jump at the base of her throat and her lips part on a gasp.

"That's two questions," she said. And then she grabbed his shirt with both hands and pulled his mouth to hers.

CHAPTER FOURTEEN

Lips and tongues collided in a firestorm of pent up desire that had only grown stronger with each passing day. It was a fury of pleasure unlike anything he'd ever known. The kiss they'd shared before had only been an appetizer, just enough to whet his appetite, and he'd been in control—mostly. But Audrey taking the reins could destroy him.

Her lips were made for kissing—soft and pink—the top lip slightly fuller than the bottom. He gave in to his earlier temptation and his teeth nipped at the plump curve. Her intake of breath was sharp and his tongue licked out to soothe it. But she wasn't going to be outdone. She was his equal in every way but physical strength, and she wasn't going to let him forget it.

Her lips slanted over his and her moan reverberated through his whole body, settling like an electric shock over his cock. He jerked her hips against him, so she could feel just how much power she had. Her hands tightened in his hair, holding him captive as she devoured his lips.

"Tent," he managed to get out. He wasn't sure his lungs were working, but his brain still had enough thought in it to know they needed protection from the cold, despite how much heat their bodies were generating. He didn't care to get frostbite on that particular part on his anatomy.

His only regret was that he wouldn't get to feel her fully naked beneath him this first time. He'd dreamed of kissing every inch of her delectable body, and then having her return the favor. The thought of having her mouth around his cock, sucking him down as she stared at him out of those big brown eyes had made him come so hard his knees had almost buckled in the shower that morning.

Audrey knew she was being reckless, but she didn't care. Somewhere between arguing with him and touching her lips to his, the dam broke inside of her and there was no way to put it back together again. Not until she had him rocking high and deep into her.

SIZZLE

She jumped up and hitched her legs around his waist, the hard length of his cock pressing directly against the drenched folds of her pussy, and his hands clamped on her ass, bringing her closer.

She felt the earth move and realized he was carrying her toward the tent. "Don't stop, Archer. Whatever you do—please don't stop."

"I couldn't if I tried, sweetheart."

They'd had a conversation a few days before, where they'd spoken of those moments in life where everything came into sharp focus—where the body became one with the universe and there was clarity where there hadn't been before. *This* was that moment for her.

She didn't know how they made it inside the tent, or how Archer maneuvered them both so he was laying on his back on top of the sleep mat and she was straddled on top of him.

His lips dipped to the underside of her jaw, kissing a path as he worked at the zipper on her jacket for better access. She shivered as the rough scrape of his beard worked in tandem with the warmth of his mouth, the different textures sending hard tremors through her sensitized body.

"God, I need to touch you so bad," he

whispered against her skin. "All of you." His hands slipped beneath the layers she wore and she tensed as he trailed a path up her back, over her scars, and then around to the front of her torso to cup her breasts. But he didn't cringe in horror, and the lust in his eyes didn't dim.

She reached between them and jerked at the drawstring on his ski pants. He lifted his hips and she yanked them past his hips, and then she did she same with the insulated long johns he wore beneath. The heavy ridge of his cock pressed snugly against his white briefs, and she licked her lips as she slowly pulled them down.

Her breath caught at the sight of him, and she felt his tremor beneath her touch. "Are you cold?"

"I've never been so fucking hot in my life."

The flesh beneath her fingers was intimidating—flushed dark with pulsing veins, a creamy drop of semen beaded at the tip. The hunger to taste him rose up inside of her, beating like a drum beneath her skin, and her mouth watered in anticipation.

"Mmm," she said, pushing his shirt up so his tight abs and the muscular indentations just above his hipbones were exposed. His chest was covered in a smattering of light blonde hair, but the muscle definition in his chest couldn't be hidden. She'd always loved the male body, and one in peak form made her want to purr.

She wanted to eat him alive. He tried to pull her back up, but she fought against his hold.

"I'll come if you do it," he rasped. "I'm too close."

"I guess I'll have to punish you for it later." She lowered her head and took a small taste of his rigid flesh and it exploded through her system. She wasn't a virgin, and she'd never been shy about her enjoyment of sex, but she never realized how much of a turn on it was to pleasure her partner. To watch him lose control.

His body jerked when her mouth closed over the plump head of his cock, and his hands fisted in the blankets beneath them. He was like a drug, making her dizzy with the addiction of his taste— slightly salty and all male.

"Have mercy, sweetheart," he groaned. "You're pushing me past my limits. I want to be deep inside that sweet pussy, feeling you clench around me when I finally come." His eyes were slitted as he looked down the length of his body to where she lay and she could see the thump of his heart pounding away in his chest.

Her smile was sly as she met his gaze. "I told you not to call me sweetheart." Her mouth surrounded his cock and she tucked her tongue beneath the sensitive flesh of the engorged head, and she almost laughed in triumph as his hips arched against her mouth and he let out a loud groan.

"Fuck—" He watched as her lips stretched wide over his cock and her fingers wrapped around the rigid stalk. Her mouth was a fucking miracle, and he swore she was stealing his mind and soul with every lick—leaving him weak and helpless like she was his own personal Kryptonite.

Despite the cold, sweat coated his skin and he could see the steam rising from their bodies. His balls drew up tight and he could feel the orgasm tingling up his spine. Before she could counteract his move, he had her flat on her back on the bedroll, her look of surprise almost comical at how fast the tables had turned.

"My turn," he said. And before she could argue he had the tie of her pants undone and stripped down her legs, taking her long johns and underwear with it in one fell swoop.

He pulled the blanket over them and then buried his face between her thighs, his tongue delving through the damp folds of her pussy and zeroing in on the taut bud of her clit.

She screamed and her hands clenched in his hair, but he didn't hold back. He knew giving her time to think would be the worst thing he could do. He'd felt her tense when she'd lost control of the situation, but as soon as his tongue licked through the thick syrup of her desire she'd become pliant as putty beneath him.

"Wait—oh, God."

"Not in a million years," he rasped. The dark curls that covered her sex were damp with need, and her flesh quivered and pulsed as he ran a finger through her juices and pushed inside of her.

Her back arched and her fingers dug into his skull and he felt the tale-tell tremors ripple along his finger. His mouth went back to work, his tongue wrapping around her clit, suckling it in a steady motion and then flicking it rapidly when he felt her getting closer to orgasm.

Her breaths came in ragged pants and he saw the tears of desperation gathered at the corners of her eyes. He couldn't wait any longer—couldn't prolong the pleasure. He rose between her thighs, his cock thick and heavy, menacing as it bobbed over her entrance.

He dropped down on his arms so he was poised over her and he slid the length of his cock up and down—down and back up—through the moist cradle of her pussy lips. His eyes were locked to hers and in them he swore he could see the soul he thought he'd lost long ago.

"Don't tease, Archer. Please—"

He pressed forward until the head of his cock was surrounded by the hottest, tightest pussy he'd ever felt. Audrey's muscles clamped around him and sweat beaded on his brow. And then he remembered—

"Please tell me you're on the pill," he panted.

She licked her lips and her fingers clenched into his buttocks. "Agency regulations," she nodded, referring to the birth control shots all female agents were given in case they were ever captured and sexually assaulted.

"Thank Christ for that," he said, and plunged deep.

Audrey threw her head back with a cry of pleasure. It had been so long, and she'd almost forgotten the pleasure of having the weight of a man pressing her down. But no one had ever filled her as Archer did, and she adjusted her hips and wrapped her legs so her ankles crossed at the small of his back to make his passage easier.

She'd forgotten how to breathe. She'd forgotten the stretching, burning, and the pleasure/pain as the body was invaded abruptly. The swollen head of his cock touched the deepest part of her, and it wasn't all together comfortable at first. He held still, the muscles in his arms straining as he held himself over her.

"Archer," she whispered.

And he was lost. Being inside of her, feeling her hot and wet around him, was as close to heaven as he ever expected to get. Her vaginal muscles rippled around him and he groaned as he felt the come boil in his balls. He wouldn't last long. Not this time.

He pulled out almost all the way and then plunged back, deep and hard, lifting her hips from the ground. And then he did it again and again with a power and ferocity that had her screaming his name in pleasure.

Her fingers searched for purchase along his back, her nails digging into his flesh. But he didn't mind the sharp bite of pain. Her head thrashed back and forth, the words tumbling from her lips a mixture of pleas and denial. She was holding back, denying her body the release it needed, though he wondered if she realized that's what she was doing.

Tears of frustration streamed down her cheeks as he built her higher and higher with no result.

"Look at me, Audrey," he whispered, his cheek pressed against hers. He leaned back and watched as her eyes fluttered open, stubbornness and fear raging in the dark depths. "Let go, sweetheart. I'll catch you when you fall."

He took her lips in a soul-searing kiss and groaned as he felt her pussy tightening around his flesh, the tremors squeezing him, demanding his own release. But he'd be damned if he didn't see to her satisfaction before he found his own. Even if it killed him.

He unwrapped her legs from around his waist and pushed them higher, so her legs rested over his shoulders and his penetration was even deeper. Their bodies were slicked with sweat and their breaths labored, but he didn't stop, his tongue dancing and thrusting with hers as her mewls of pleasure grew louder.

And then he felt it. The rush of liquid and her muscles squeezing him so tightly he groaned through the pleasure. Her screams filled the tent and her nails raked down his back as the orgasm destroyed her.

Archer couldn't hold on any longer and let himself go, slamming himself against her one last time. Hot streams of cum shot from his cock and filled her. He wanted to mark her. Brand her. So there would be no doubt that she was his. But he realized almost before the thought was complete that she'd branded him just as deeply. He was hers.

To hell with everything he thought he'd known about relationships before. It all paled in comparison. His body collapsed on top of her, his breathing labored against her neck where her pulse beat wildly. Her hands slipped from his back and she turned her head into him.

Her kiss was soft and subtle, barely a whisper against his cheek, but the sweetness of it caught him off guard and filled him with a tenderness he'd never felt toward a lover before. He wanted to take care of her, to coddle her and keep her safe. And she was the last woman on earth who needed a man for that.

He pulled out of her slowly, his cock still sensitive even though he was only semi-erect, and he rolled to the side, pulling her into his arms and tugging the blankets up around them. They'd only be able to stay like this until the cold broke through the heat they'd created, but for now it was nice just to hold each other.

"I think we're in trouble here, sweetheart."

She didn't even correct him this time as he said the endearment, and he looked down to see her dark eyelashes resting against her pale skin. She was already fast asleep. Her mind might not trust him yet, but her body sure as hell did.

CHAPTER FIFTEEN

They dozed on and off for a couple of hours, finally getting up to put clothes back on when the temperature got too cold. Archer grabbed a couple of bottles of water and some trail mix and brought it back into the tent, while Audrey straightened the blankets. His mouth quirked when he saw she'd moved the bedrolls so they lay side by side and spread their covers on top. It wasn't the Ritz, but it looked cozy, and just the thought of stretching out beside her had his cock twitching in anticipation.

"I looked around while I was getting the food," he said, handing the supplies over to her. "The structure is sound enough and there's enough ventilation that I think we could get away with having a small fire. The floor is dirt, so I could dig a pit and just use some of the scrap wood as a starter.

We could move the tent closer and leave the flap open."

"You just want to be able to get naked again and not freeze your balls off," she said with a grin. "You can't fool me."

"If you'll gather the wood, we can be done twice as fast. And I'll let you be on top this time."

"You're an excellent negotiator. I can see why Declan hired you."

He laughed and they left the tent to see to their tasks of building a fire. Archer dug a trench in the dirt and found some old pieces of metal that had once been part of a hearth up against the wall. Or what had once been a wall.

It didn't take long for the pit to form and Audrey stacked wood, leaving plenty of room for ventilation beneath and for the bits of tinder he'd stuffed in his pack from Joe's store. He pushed it beneath the wood and used the survival lighter to start a small flame. It didn't take long for the dry wood to catch and before long there was a nice blaze going.

Audrey repositioned the tent as close as it was safe to and opened the flaps wide. And then his mouth watered as she started to strip out of her clothes.

"A deal's a deal, right?"

"I always keep my word," he said soberly.

"Good. Now get naked. Word on the street is I get to be on top this time."

"I make it a point never to argue with an armed woman." He stripped out of his jacket and laid it close to the fire and then did the same with his other clothes. "I've got to confess, I've never made love to a woman before while she was wearing her Glock inside her coat pocket. Something like that could scare off a lesser man."

She arched a brow and looked down at his hardening cock. "I'm not sure I could handle any *more* of a man."

"Are you sure you want to be on top this time?" he asked. "Because I have the sudden urge to bend you over that pack and sink right between the round globes of that pretty ass. Have I mentioned how much I love your ass?"

"You've brought it up a time or two. That's a pretty dominant position," she said, naked except for the plain undershirt she wore instead of a bra. Cotton had never looked so sexy. She looked him over from head to toe, lingering at the hard flesh between his thighs. "I think it's a position you have to earn, but you'll be the first to know."

He grinned at her cockiness and he moved toward her until the tip of his cock brushed against the cotton of her shirt. "You're playing with fire, sweetheart," he said, leaning down to nip at her bottom lip. "Because when I finally get you on your hands and knees, it's going to be more than you bargained for."

His hands reached around to cup the globes of her ass, and he trailed a finger down the cleft and circled the puckered rosebud of her back entrance.

"Have you ever been taken here?" he whispered against her lips. He dipped his fingers lower, gathering the sweet syrup of her desire, and then bringing it back up to the other passage. The tip of his finger pushed past the tight resistance and she moaned with pleasure.

"Have you, Audrey? Do you know what it feels like to be stretched around a man's cock, to be completely at his mercy as he fucks you in a forbidden place?"

"No," she panted. "I've never—"

He growled low as the vision invaded his mind of her spread before him, his dick buried deep inside her ass, as she gave him something she'd never given another man.

"It's the ultimate act of trust," he said, pushing his finger a little deeper and then bringing it back out to gather more of her juices before returning. He worked one finger, then two, stretching her as she flexed around him. "You have to have complete faith in your partner to prepare you properly. But the pleasure—"

He bent his legs slightly and lifted her to her toes at the same time, so his cock slid between the damp folds of her pussy. "It's unimaginable pleasure," he whispered. He pulled his fingers free and felt her deflate against him. "So make sure you tell me as soon as I've earned the dominant position."

"You're good at distracting me," she said, taking a step back. "It's my turn. Don't think I've forgotten."

"Are you going to take that shirt off, or are you going to keep hiding them from me? Because I've seen the scars. And they don't seem to have any effect at all on how hard my cock is. If you get to be on top then I should at least get the pleasure of seeing those lovely breasts bouncing. Have I mentioned that I love your breasts almost as much as your ass?" he asked with a grin.

She laughed—she couldn't remember anyone who'd ever made her laugh as much as Archer. She pulled the tank top over her head, standing before him, scars and all. His eyes darkened and his cock flexed against his stomach. For the first time since she'd gotten them, they ceased to exist, because the wicked hunger in his eyes was enough to make her feel whole.

"Lay down," she said, pointing to the mat she'd moved closer to the fire.

He did as she asked and the corner of his mouth tilted up in a smirk. "You'd better get over here and warm me up. It's still pretty fucking cold even with the fire."

She ducked into the tent and knelt between his spread legs, enjoying the way he watched her. Her breasts felt heavy and she cupped them with her hands, her thumbs skimming across her sensitive nipples, and her head dropped back with pleasure.

"Not fair," he rasped. "I want to play too."

Her hand dipped down to the curls covering her sex and she could feel the moist heat before her fingers delved between the folds. She was wet, more than ready to take him, but she felt the ache from their earlier lovemaking. She'd be lucky if she could walk if they kept up this pace.

"Some day that smart mouth of yours is going to get you into trouble."

"Promises, promises—"

She slid up his body until she straddled his hips, and she leaned forward so her nipples scraped across the hair on his chest. Her teeth nipped at his lips and then she whispered, "Here's a promise for you. I'm going to ride you until it's my name you're screaming. Better hold on."

Audrey poised herself over the head of his cock and sank down to the hilt, reveling in the harsh groan that escaped his lips. And then she did exactly what she'd promised and rode him with everything she had—as if it were the last pleasure they'd ever have.

She held onto his hands, using them as an anchor, as she rolled her hips in a way that had beads of sweat popping out on his brow. She showed no mercy. Her focus on him was so complete that her own orgasm took her completely by surprise when it came upon her. Electrical pulses exploded from her clit and sizzled through her body, and she threw her head back and rode out the storm.

He swelled inside of her seconds before he called out her name, and she felt the flood of his release deep inside of her.

Even with the fire, they couldn't stay unclothed for long, so they pulled on the insulated long johns and thick socks and burrowed under the covers. Audrey could've slept for a week, she felt so drained. It had been a long time since she'd been that relaxed.

They lay in silence for a long while, but she could feel him thinking and wondered what was keeping him awake.

"Do you remember the face of the Syrian who tortured you?" he finally said, staring at the top of the tent.

The question surprised her, but she didn't hesitate to answer. Something was weighing heavily on his mind. "I see him in my nightmares. His name was Farid. He always insisted that I call him by name. But I never did. I never spoke at all."

Archer pulled her closer so her head was tucked beneath his chin, and she tried to relax. But just saying Farid's name brought his face to mind— the complete and utter peace that had been on it every time he'd taken a hot iron to her ribs. She sometimes thought she could still smell her burning flesh.

"You asked about Warlock earlier," he said. "Warlock was that man. Like your Farid."

Audrey froze against him in shock, but she stayed silent. She felt the tightness of his body, the rigidness of his muscles, as he found the courage to tell her about his past. And she deliberately relaxed against him, hoping he would be at ease. He kissed the top of her head absentmindedly while she stroked his chest in comfort.

"The government gives media spin about how humane the agencies are. How we don't torture our enemies. But it's all bullshit. They tell you it's for the greater good. That the secrets we're extracting will save the human race as we know it. And it's true for the most part."

"You don't have to explain yourself to me, Archer. I know and understand better than anyone. Our jobs aren't always pretty. But we do them as we see fit because it's never just one person at risk."

"But it eventually takes a toll on the mind and the body. Especially the job that I had—that Warlock had," he corrected. "There's always a turning point in that particular line of work where you either cross the line and become that person forever—the kind of person who can torture and kill without a second thought. They either end up eating their own bullet because of the terrible things they've done, or they take a step back and decide to walk away from it all. Try to start over. Either way, in life or in death, the horror of it follows. You can never outrun it."

"No, but you can survive it," she said, beginning to understand him a little bit better. "And you were one who was able to walk away."

"Did you know it was our team that was sent in to gather intel on where Osama Bin Laden was being hidden?"

"No, but I could've guessed. They'd have sent in the best."

"It was me and Dec and Cypher. Gabe Brennan had already retired and Kane Huxley was supposedly dead, so our five man team was already down to three. We each had our jobs. Dec's like the wind. He blends so seamlessly that you never even realize he's there until it's too late. Cypher worked the tech. And I was the muscle. My job was to get as much information as possible so we could feed it to SEAL Team 6."

Archer didn't mention that the team was commanded by Shane MacKenzie. The identities of that particular team were fiercely guarded because of all the high stakes missions they'd accomplished.

"Timing was crucial, and I did my job exactly how I was supposed to on a high ranking official of Al Qaida." He held up his hand and flexed it into a fist. "I know just where to hit to cause the most pain without rendering them unconscious. I broke him in eight hours and got all the information we needed. And then I happened to look up in time to catch my reflection in a shard of glass left over from a broken mirror that was hanging on the wall. I didn't even recognize the eyes staring back at me.

"Then I thought of my daughter and wondered what she'd think of her father in that moment. I turned in my resignation as soon as I made it back stateside. Good timing on my part, as Declan had already been setting up MacKenzie Security and had everything in place. I didn't know it was going to be his last mission too, but he didn't have to try very hard to convince me to join him." He let out a long breath as if a weight had been lifted from his chest.

"I'd follow Dec into hell and back. I *have* followed him into hell and back. And eventually, maybe the good we're doing now will make up for the person I was while working for the CIA. Warlock's death was the best thing that ever happened to me. Until you."

He kissed her on top of the head again and she moved so it was her lips he met instead. Audrey had felt many emotions during her thirty years—fear, lust, anger—but not love. She realized what had been blooming before Jonah had tried to kill her was nothing in comparison to what she felt for Archer. He was a man she'd walk beside proudly, in battle and out. And if they made it out of this mess alive, she promised herself that she would tell him.

CHAPTER SIXTEEN

By noon the next day, the backs of both of their necks were itching and a restlessness had settled over their camp.

Audrey appreciated that Archer could go from pleasure to business in the blink of an eye. They'd spent most of the night talking and making love— and boy, she was feeling the aches in her muscles— but when dawn had come they'd gone about their routine. She'd scouted the perimeter while he saw to the food for the dogs and took them out to get a little exercise.

"It's clear," she said once she ducked back inside the abandoned saloon that had become an unofficial headquarters. "There's nothing for miles. And no tracks but ours. But—"

"You've got a feeling," Archer said, finishing her sentence. "And it's a bad one."

"Yeah. We should have brought more firepower."

Archer stood in front of the table where she'd laid out all their weapons. They were each carrying their personal pieces, but there were backups, plenty of magazines, a couple of hand grenades, and the two H&K MP5 submachine guns.

She'd stripped out of her heavy coat, leaving her only in the black ski pants and the matching thermal top. She braided her hair and pulled a black watch cap low over her ears. Archer was dressed identically to her. Neither of them wanted to have to fight with the weight of extra clothing if they needed to move quickly.

The sat phone buzzed against the warped wooden table and Archer hit the button so it was on speaker. Declan's voice filled the room.

"You've got incoming heat, and they're moving fast. Cyph was finally able to get the satellite imaging up and running."

"Get off my balls, man," Cal said. "I had to hack through NASA and the Pentagon to get them, but I'm your eyes now."

"It looks like they sent a six man team and they're about five kilometers out," Dec said.

"Shit, they're practically right on top of us." Archer pulled the strap of the MP5 over his shoulder and let it hang in front of him.

Audrey grabbed extra magazines from the table and took the other MP5, though she didn't bother with the strap because it would only get in her way.

"We can use the area to our advantage," Archer said. "We've been here long enough to get acclimated."

"We need to split up," she said, knowing how his mind worked well enough to guess the game plan. "One of the buildings across the street has good coverage. I'll take point there."

Archer pocketed the two grenades and checked the magazine in his Glock, putting it in his pocket when he saw it was only half full. He grabbed another and popped it in, chambering a bullet.

"I'm going to set the dogs loose. Joe said they were trained to find their way home. I don't want them caught here."

Adrenaline pumped through her system with the force of a thousand men. The dogs were their only transportation. Without them they were going to have a hell of a time tracking down Salt. But there wasn't time to argue, and she knew he was right, so she nodded and took off out the front door to the building she'd marked on the opposite side of the street.

***

Archer released the dogs and gave them the command Joe had told him to send them home, and he barely made it back under cover before he heard the low buzz of engines in the distance.

"Keep the link open," Declan demanded. "We can see their shoe size from here and they're packing major heat."

Archer could tell as soon as the first snowmobile appeared at the edge of town that these were a different caliber of agents than the ones who had held Audrey in the warehouse. He watched in silence through a rotted hole in the wall, and then swore as two of the agents peeled off and went behind the buildings.

The good news was that everything was in close quarters. He could throw a rock and hit one of the buildings across the street. The lane between the two sides was narrow, and the Russians would be sitting ducks if they came down that way.

"Oh, shit," he whispered as one of the agents hefted a rocket launcher and settled it on his shoulder.

The Russian didn't know where he and Audrey were hiding, but that didn't matter. His goal was to smoke them out, get them out in the open. And it was a pretty effective way of doing so.

Before the man could get a shot off, Archer moved outside of the building and pulled the pin on the grenade in his hand, launching it toward the enemy. He'd just given away his position, but it was sure as hell better to take the offensive than having to dodge rockets.

The four agents scattered like bowling pins as soon as they saw the grenade, and the explosion rattled the fragile building that was his only protection. Gunfire erupted and he knew without looking that Audrey had the sub on full auto and was laying down cover so the Russian with the rocket launcher couldn't get that shot off.

"You've got two heat signals coming from the opposite end of town," Cypher said through the phone.

As long as Audrey kept laying down cover, he could take care of the others coming in. He caught them by surprise, moving quickly so he was almost perpendicular with them when he took them down. Two quick rounds to the chest and the enemy was now four instead of six.

The Russians were returning Audrey's fire now, having found their own places for cover, and he made his way back up the strip. A man stepped out in front of him, so close there wasn't room to get his gun up in time, and he barely ducked back as the blade of a knife swiped toward his middle.

He didn't feel the cut along his side, but he smelled the blood. Archer grabbed the man's wrist and twisted, hearing the satisfying crunch of bone as his fingers went limp and the knife dropped to the ground. Another punch to the throat killed the man instantly. He kept moving forward, toward Audrey.

A body lay prone in the middle of the lane, the snow beneath him bright crimson. But Archer's blood turned cold and his heart stopped in his chest when he heard Audrey's yell and the sound of the rocket launcher as it fired straight at the building she was using for cover.

He started running. And praying. And he watched with amazement as Audrey's body shot out of the building just before the rocket hit, curling up in a ball at the last minute so she rolled out into the middle of the lane as the building exploded behind her.

The two remaining agents stepped out of their hiding places, their weapons trained on her, and all he could think was that he couldn't lose her. Not like this.

He sprinted to the bigger of the two men and knocked the gun up just as he was about to fire, so the bullet went wild into the sky. This agent was better at hand to hand than the other, and didn't let Archer get in too close. They were evenly matched and it was only hearing similar sounds of combat coming from Audrey and the other agent that had him taking a chance to reach into his boot and pull the knife, striking it between the man's ribs and into his heart before he could deliver his own killing blow.

***

Audrey couldn't show weakness. Couldn't let her guard down. Blood dripped into her eye from the cut above her eyebrow and she wiped at it quickly as she dodged a punch from the man who'd fired the rocket launcher.

She knew how to fight. Knew that concentration and focus was the most important thing. But something broke through that concentration, and before she could blink the man had her in a headlock, her breath cut off and her lungs burning. Blood rushed in her ears, muting the sounds around her, but she realized with complete clarity what had broken through her focus.

It wasn't the static of the sat phone from somewhere in the distance and Declan's frantic warnings. But the pitched tune of Pop Goes the Weasel being whistled in a rather upbeat tempo.

It was that moment she knew she was going to die—the arm around her throat was cutting off the oxygen to her brain, but it was Jonah Salt whistling from just over the hill who would deliver the killing blow.

The man holding her captive jerked behind her and his arm loosened around her throat, so she was able to greedily suck in air. The report of a rifle had been close and she managed to get a glimpse of the man who'd held her, a neat bullet hole right in the center of his forehead.

"Down," Archer yelled. But her brain and her reaction time was slow. She felt his body jerk as he knocked her to the ground, his body covering hers as the sound of another shot being fired penetrated the fog in her brain.

"Get up! Get up!" She knew he'd been hit, but he had her up on her feet, his body hunched over hers for protection as he ushered her back toward the safety of the buildings.

CHAPTER SEVENTEEN

"What the hell was that?" Declan said through the open line once they made it back to home base. "I've got six bodies on the ground and then a heat signal comes out of fucking nowhere and starts laying down rifle fire."

"It was Salt." Audrey's voice was barely discernable and Archer handed her a bottle of water. "I heard him."

"I'm sorry, what?" Dec asked.

"He whistles while he works. He always has. The sound of it broke my concentration and that Russian agent almost snapped my neck."

"And then Salt shot him and saved you?" Cal asked. "That makes no sense."

"It's part of the game," Archer said, looking at her intently. "He wanted her to know he was there. That he was the one pulling the trigger. He killed the immediate threat so she'd know."

"That is fucked up," Cal said, "But I've got his heat signature now. I'm following him back to wherever he was hiding. And he's moving at a fast clip. He's got a snowmobile. I'll be able to find his hiding place and then you'll have the coordinates you need to find him."

"You guys okay?" Declan asked.

Audrey looked at the blood that covered Archer's arm and stomach, but he shook his head no at her, telling her not to mention it to Declan. He dug around in their supplies and came out with the First Aid kit and then stripped off his shirt.

"We're fine. Nothing we can't patch up with the First Aid kit."

Audrey raised her eyebrows at that statement, thinking it might be a little overzealous. She moved closer and took the kit from his hands and then pointed with her finger, telling him to sit without words.

He leaned in and kissed her softly on the lips, and then pulled back to look at the cut over her eye.

"It's fine," she whispered. "But you're going to need stitches."

He grunted and sat down where she pointed while she went about gathering the supplies she needed—fresh water and wood for a new fire.

"What the hell?" Cal said, after a few minutes of silence. "No, no, no. This can't be possible."

Dread knotted in Audrey's stomach as the rapid click of the keyboard was heard across the line, and Cal's unintelligible mutters were interspersed with a lot of *fucks*.

"He's gone," Declan said.

"What do you mean gone?" Archer asked. "He can't just disappear."

"And yet, that's exactly what it looks like from where we're standing. I was prepared for something like this."

"Maybe you should fill me in, boss, because I'm confused as hell," Archer growled out. "Why would you expect him to disappear into nothing? Unless you believe all the bullshit about it being The End of the World."

"It's close enough," Dec said. "I did some digging, and that particular area was once an underground KGB headquarters. It was completely off the books and functional up until 1991 when the KGB disbanded. That coincides with the timeline of the last couple who disappeared from that area—a man and woman who were self-proclaimed adventurers. More than likely they got too close and were captured. The KGB would have made their bodies disappear for good."

"Jesus." Archer scrubbed a hand over his face and it came away with dirt and blood.

"Are the two of you secure for now?"

"Unless Salt decides to come back and play some more."

"Good. Give us a couple of hours to dig out some more information. We're close. Really close to getting a lock on all of this. Stand by."

The phone disconnected and Audrey reached over and hit the off button. "I'm sorry I dragged all of you into this."

"I can't think of a better choice," he said, lips quirking. "I'm just glad I found you when I did. You couldn't have continued to go after him alone. Not without getting yourself killed."

"No, but I would've kept going because the revenge was all I could see."

"And now?" he asked.

She smiled and knelt down by the fire, lighting the tinder and listening to the wood crackle a moment before she answered him. "And now things are a little clearer. I'm grateful for the help. You're a good partner."

"You're not so bad yourself, Sharpe. Just think how good we'll be together twenty years from now."

Her hands froze inside the First Aid box and she didn't have the courage to look up at his face to see what he meant by that statement. Instead she relaxed and pulled out bandages and a needle and thread. "If I'm still working in the field twenty years from now, I give you permission to go ahead and put a bullet in my head. The body can only take so much wear and tear."

She'd put the bottles of water next to the fire, hoping it would warm them some, but it wasn't going to be warm enough.

"Like I said, I've got this great little place down in Costa Rica. A private beach and a view unlike any other. Let me know the second you start thinking about retirement and I'll buy the plane tickets."

"This is going to be cold," she said, grabbing one of the water bottles and a clean cloth. The wound on his arm and across his stomach had to be cleaned before she could sew him back up.

"I've had worse," he shrugged. "Just get it done."

So that's what she did. She cleaned the areas as thoroughly as she could, relieved to see the bullet had passed through the outer edge of his tricep, barely a scratch mark really. But it was still deep enough to need several stitches. The cut along his stomach was long and red, but it would be fine with butterfly bandages and antiseptic.

"Thanks for pushing me down." Her throat was raw and it was harder for her to speak than it had been just a few minutes earlier. The area around her throat where the man's arm had been was swollen and tender to the touch. "I knew the second the bullet was fired and hit the man holding me that there'd be another one for me. I thought that was the end, you know? I was just waiting for it."

Audrey took a long drink of cold water, hoping that would soothe the burn. Archer's hand came up and cupped her cheek gently and she leaned against it.

"It's never over until you give up." He brought

his lips to hers, rubbing softly, his tongue licking along the seam until she opened for him. It wasn't a kiss of high passion—the flash and bang of what they'd shared the night before. This was an easing into each other—an acceptance. He pulled back and smiled. "I wasn't ready to give up yet. Not when I've just found you."

She nodded because that's all she could do, and then she went about the task of sewing up his arm. It didn't take long, but it was never an easy process to stick a needle through flesh over and over again without deadening the area. By the time she was finished and wrapped gauze around the wound, sweat had beaded on Archer's brow and he was shivering from the cold.

"Get some clean clothes on and get warm."

"I will if you'll let me take care of that cut above your eyebrow. You'll keep opening it up and bleeding if I don't close it."

She nodded in agreement and passed over the supplies. His hands were gentle as he put butterfly bandages across the cut.

"I've got a confession to make," he said once he was finished. His fingers trailed down her jaw and glanced over the line of bruises across her neck, and she watched his face darken with anger.

"What's that?" she croaked out.

He met her gaze and the heat there almost knocked her over with its intensity. "Watching you dive out of the front of that building as it exploded was one of the hottest things I've seen in my entire life. If you weren't injured right now, you'd be flat on your back in the dirt."

"Promises, promises," she said, mimicking him from the night before.

"You're trouble, Agent Sharpe."

"Punish me later." She leaned forward and nipped at his lower lip just as the sat phone started buzzing again.

CHAPTER EIGHTEEN

"It's time to lock and load," Cal said excitedly on the other end of the line. "I cracked that bitch wide open. This is the moment where you all should be congratulating me."

"Why don't you tell us what you did first and then I'll send you a fruit basket," Archer said.

"Why do you want me to explain? You won't understand any of it anyway."

"You and I are due a round in the ring, my friend."

"Bring it on, buttercup. I've got youth on my side."

"You're only two years younger than I am.

You're not exactly the picture of youth."

"I'll take whatever advantage I can get. Your fists are like ham hocks. Hurts like a bitch."

"I'm sorry," Audrey interrupted. "But you were talking about breaking a bitch wide open. Maybe you could expound on that a bit. Unless Archer is the bitch."

Archer shot her a look of retribution but she just grinned back. Dec had made the right call. She'd fit right in at MacKenzie Security.

"Damn, I think I'm going to love you, Agent Sharpe," Cal said. "Now listen close, because we're going to be working on a time clock here. Salt has set up the system at the KGB base to piggyback off the CIA's mainframe. It's actually an ingenious way to go undetected. He knows the codes and the timing, so if those bombs detonate, it'll be traced back to U.S. soil. He's got worldwide catastrophe at the ends of his fingertips."

"So how do we keep him from blowing the tankers? I'm assuming he'll know the moment we get near. He has to have infrared technology in a place like that."

"I've got you covered. I was able to piggyback off his piggyback, if that makes any sense. I'm running the shots as long as I'm tapped in. But here's the problem. The detonators are set to explode automatically if he doesn't log in and type in a password every six hours. It's a failsafe in case something happens to him."

"Lovely," Audrey sighed out.

"I can shut down his sensors without him knowing before you get into range, but I'm close to being able to reprogram the detonation codes so the ones he has will be inactive. I've programmed the route he took into your watches. I'll follow your progress from here."

"So we're basically walking into the lion's den without knowing how to get through the doors?" Archer asked.

"I'm still working on that part. Just get moving. By my estimation, he's got a little over an hour before he needs to check in and type in the codes. Make sure you're wearing your comm units. The sat phone won't be viable once you cross a certain point."

"It must be nice to be sitting behind a computer screen a couple thousand miles away right now."

"I'm not complaining," Cal said.

"Don't worry," Dec cut in. "He's up in the

rotation for the next assignment."

"It'll probably be guarding some heiress in a five-star hotel somewhere. Bastard has all the luck."

"You know how much I hate the cold," Cal said deadpan. "She's lucky she got you for this round."

"I'd say so," Audrey chimed in. "I would've already put a bullet in you by now."

Archer barked out a laugh and watched the smile tug at Audrey's lips. "Signing out and turning comm units on. Watch our backs out there. He's not going to play nice."

"Roger that."

Audrey checked her watch as it beeped and coordinates began coming through, and then she took the earpiece Archer handed her and put it in her ear.

"Checking in with control," Archer said.

"Reading you loud and clear. You guys keep the mushy talk to a minimum. I don't want to lose my lunch all over Miranda."

"I'm pretty sure you lost your virginity all over Miranda. I'm sure a little lunch won't bother her a bit."

"Fuck you, Archer."

"That means I won that round," he whispered to Audrey.

They collected weapons and checked ammo, and put on their heavy jackets and hats for the ride.

"I'm assuming we're going to commandeer our dead Russian friends' snowmobiles to make the trek to The End of the World."

"I think they'd want us to have them," Archer said, spinning the MR5 around so it hung on his back. "You ready."

She nodded and followed him outside, ignoring the bodies that still littered the ground. Three of the snowmobiles had been destroyed by Archer's grenade, but they found two that were in good shape.

Jonah had been out riding quite a bit if the snowmobile tracks were anything to show for it. They used the coordinates on their watches to keep on course, and the watch buzzed as soon as they hit their destination.

"We've got a small problem here, Cyph," Archer said. "We're at the end of our destination and there is nothing here but snow. A lot of snow. There are snowmobile tracks all across and back again, but there's nothing else."

"It's an underground KGB bunker. You're standing right on top of it. Now we just have to figure out how to get you in."

"You don't know how?" he asked incredulously.

"I'm working on it. You guys always expect the impossible, and nothing is ever that easy."

"My apologies. Just take your time while we stand here and twiddle our thumbs."

"I do have good news," Cal said. "I broke the codes for his antipersonnel explosives so the ones he has are no longer operable. Declan's making the call to the SEALs so they can locate the ships and remove the devices. He wants you to bring Salt in."

"What?" Audrey asked, the color draining from her face. "That's not acceptable. He dies here. Today."

"I'm just relaying orders. If you can bring him in alive, then do so. The CIA has gotten wind somehow that Salt is alive. We think your Russian intelligence boys tipped them off to complicate things."

"We'll deal with it when it comes to that," Archer said, reaching over to squeeze Audrey's hand, but she was like a statue and he could see the pain on her face. "Tell me how to get inside and find him."

"There's some type of voice activation code, but it's not anything I recognize. It's not an actual voice command, but it's got a high frequency and pitch. Miranda isn't picking it up yet, but we're filtering it through the system."

"You think it's electronic?"

"That could be a possibility."

"No," Audrey said. "It won't be electronic." And then she started to whistle the same tune Salt had whistled while shooting at her earlier. It was just another part of his game.

The ground trembled beneath their feet and the snow shifted as stairs that led into the earth seemed to appear from nowhere. Audrey and Archer both reached for their weapons and spread out from each other, trying to keep their balance as the ground continued to shake.

She heard the answering whistle as Salt appeared at the top of the stairs and she raised her gun.

"I wondered if you'd figure it out," he said, his smile sending chills down her spine. He ignored Archer completely. His eyes were only for her. "You were always a bright student. Damned hard to kill, but very bright."

"Jonah Salt," Audrey said. "You're to be transported to Langley on charges of treason and terrorism."

"No, I don't think so. You forget the little matter of the oil tankers that are set to blow. In fact," he said, checking his watch, "if I don't type in the codes to disarm them in the next eight minutes they'll detonate." He spread his hands in a gesture to indicate an explosion and said, "Boom. It'll be bad, love. It's best if you and your friend find a safe place to hide."

Salt finally looked over at Archer and his smile faded. "Oh, wait. Never mind. I've decided to kill you instead. Six feet under is as safe a place as any, I guess."

Archer let Audrey do the talking. The connection between the two of them was obvious, and he didn't want to set Salt off by interrupting.

"I've got bad news for you, Jonah. Your little devices have been deactivated. It turns out you're not quite as good at covering your tracks as you think you are."

"Don't bullshit me, Audrey. There are less than a handful of people who could decipher those codes to deactivate the entire system."

"You don't believe me? Fine. We can stand here for the next six and a half minutes and see what happens when you don't check in. I've got nowhere to be at the moment."

"Jesus, Sharpe," Cal hissed through the earpiece. "Don't antagonize him."

Salt stared Audrey down, trying to decide if she was bluffing or not, and he finally sent her a knowing smile that had ice forming in Archer's gut.

"So we're at an impasse, it seems," he said. The corners of his mouth quirked and his eyes were stone cold. "I have other projects, though this one has been very lucrative so far. If I'd known how tenacious you were going to be, love, I might have brought you in on it. You did have—" he looked her up and down with a sneer on his face, "Certain attributes that I found very enjoyable."

It took everything Archer had not to give in to the temptation and unload his weapon into the pompous ass. His arm jerked in reflex, but he kept the gun down by his side. But it was enough movement for Salt to notice.

"Ahh, that bothers you does it, Agent Ryan? Our Audrey likes to spread her favors around, so it seems."

Archer let the rage rush through him only to be replaced by ice. There was no use for anger in a volatile situation. Jonah was a master at playing games. That's all he was doing now.

"You might be wondering how I know your name, but it wasn't difficult to figure out. I know all about Archer Ryan and who you're working for. I apologize for making you cut your vacation short with your daughter. I'll make sure to send flowers for your funeral."

Salt put his hand in his pocket and Archer tensed, bringing up his weapon, but Salt only pulled out a small silver remote, no bigger than a finger.

"Relax, Agent Ryan. Or should I call you Warlock. I remember you from some years back. You had quite the reputation in the CIA. Though I'd heard rumors you'd died quite horribly."

"You know what they say about rumors," Archer said.

"So it seems. Today is just as good a day for that horrible death."

"And how do you hope to accomplish that?" Audrey asked. "Last I checked there were two of us and one of you."

"Well, first I am going to put a bullet in you. Right here," he said, pointing at his forehead. "You won't be able to walk away from that one, and I think it's important for Agent Ryan to watch you die. He cares for you, though he's trying not to show it. Really, it's very sweet." Salt's smile was a cruel slash across his face.

"And I do owe you for the shot you took on me the other day." He flexed his shoulder where the bullet had penetrated. "It was very clever of you to come at me from the water. I didn't expect it. And clever is something you've always been, Audrey. Which is just another reason it's important for you to die first."

"The minute you do he'll gun you down like the dog you are," she said coolly. "It's worth the sacrifice."

"Ahh, there's where the problem comes in," Salt said. "I've got nothing to lose here. The second my heart stops beating this whole area will blow. I've got this nifty heart monitor." He pulled back the sleeve of his jacket to expose the flesh colored pad and digital readout of his heartbeat. "And it's connected wirelessly to enough TNT to take out a good chunk of Alaska the minute my heart stops beating. So either way, the two of you die."

Archer caught Audrey's gaze and in it he saw the finality and acceptance of what was going to happen. There was a good chance that neither of them would come out of this alive.

He heard Cal and Declan talking on the other end of the ear bud, while Cal tried to figure out a way to disarm the bomb and get everyone out alive, but he knew they were worried. The calmer Declan's voice became the more worried he was.

"Audrey," he said, seeing in her eyes the sacrifice she planned to make. "Trust me."

She nodded once and looked back at Jonah. "If I'm going to die," she said, "then I plan to drag you with me kicking and screaming."

Salt let the gun drop down from his sleeve and into his hand, but Archer was ready for him. He shot him in the chest, just to the left of his heart. It was a killing blow that would have him bleeding out in seconds, but it would hopefully keep his heart pumping long enough for them to get the hell out of there.

Salt squeezed off two rounds as he crumpled to his knees, but they went wild.

"Run," Archer yelled, sprinting as fast as he could for the snowmobile.

Archer grabbed Audrey by the arm and pulled her with him to the closest one. He straddled it and started the engine as she climbed on behind him. There wasn't time to look back. His only thought was to go as fast as he could and get as far away as possible. He pressed on the accelerator and it took off, spraying snow up on both sides so it hit them in the face.

The sound of another gunshot seemed unusually loud over the engine, and he heard Audrey whisper, "Oh, God." Her arms tightened around his waist. "He shot himself in the head."

Seconds was all it took for the earth to rumble beneath them as the bomb detonated. The earth seemed to cave in on itself, starting as a small hole in the center where Jonah's body had been and rippling outward, disintegrating everything in its path as it widened.

"Faster, faster," Audrey chanted in his ear, leaning forward as if that would help with the momentum.

The rumble beneath them became louder and the vibrations made the snowmobile difficult to control. And then, as suddenly as it began, it stopped and the world seemed to go still. Audrey hugged him tight and he could feel her ragged breath against his back.

Archer skidded the snowmobile to a stop and turned to look at the destruction.

"Sweet Christ," he whispered under his breath. Not twenty feet from where they stood was a crater in the earth at least the size of two football fields. There was nothing there but a gaping hole of darkness. Truly the end of the world.

"I think I need to tell you something important," Audrey said, still clinging to his waist. He didn't want her to ever let go. That was much too close of a call.

"Yes, I'll have sex with you," he said to lighten the tension. "But give me a couple of minutes for my balls to get out of my throat. Jesus, that was close."

"Idiot." She choked out a laugh. "I was going to tell you I love you, but I think I've changed my mind."

He turned to look at her and cocked a brow. "You can't take it back, sweetheart. We just survived The End of the World."

"I'm trying not to gag here," Cal said through

the earbud.

"Shut up, Cyph. I'd like to tell the woman I love her without your help."

"Buddy, you need all the help you can get."

"I've got all the help I need right here in my arms." He pulled the piece out of his ear and tossed it into the snow, and then he pulled Audrey into his arms and kissed her laughing mouth. The End of the World was a good place to start a future.

CHAPTER NINETEEN

Two Months Later…

The sun beat down on her face as she watched the waves crash along the shore. Her toes itched to be in the sand, and she wanted to feel the water lap against her legs.

After Alaska, she wasn't sure she'd ever be warm again. Then she'd been stuck in Montana for almost six weeks—where it was still cold and snowing—so she could be debriefed by her old CIA handler and fill out paperwork that officially released her to work for MacKenzie Security. She was now gainfully employed, and it felt a little odd considering the life she'd led the past years.

Once all the details had been taken care of,

Archer had told Declan that he still owed him vacation days, and he'd whisked her away to his home in Costa Rica. Where she'd finally gotten warm.

His home was beautiful—the roof was orange tile and the walls a pale stucco. It was open and airy with lots of windows to enjoy the view, and it was hidden behind an iron gate and lush trees that hid parrots and the occasional monkey. It was an oasis of complete privacy and seclusion, and the ocean was so close she only had to walk out the back door and down the short flight of stairs to be on the beach and in the water.

As soon as she'd walked inside his home, she'd felt the tension leave her shoulders. It had *felt* like home. And she felt like she had a purpose again— one that she could be proud of and a partner who would stand beside her always. He stimulated her mind and her body in equal measure.

She watched with pleasure as Archer stretched out on the padded lounger down by the water. They'd spent the last week being as lazy as possible—making love and taking longs naps before making love again. She knew his habits by now— how he woke early and ran up and down the beach for miles and then came back for his first cup of coffee and shower.

And every afternoon, he'd change into his swim trunks and take a book, or nothing at all, and lay out on the cushioned lounger by the water, soaking in the sun and dozing in the tropical heat.

Just seeing him laid out as he was made her mouth water. He was beautiful to look at, his skin browned by the sun and his hard abs and chest glistening from the heat. She patted the object in the pocket of her cover-up and took a deep breath before taking the stairs down to the beach.

His face was slack with sleep and his breathing even. She unzipped the cover-up and then quickly undid the ties of her bathing suit, letting it fall to the sand. She moved quietly beside him, straddling her knees on either side of his leg, and then she worked at the tie holding up his swim trunks.

It didn't take long to loosen them and spread open the front so his flaccid penis was exposed. It wasn't often she got to see him like this, completely relaxed and pliable beneath her touch. He wouldn't be that way for long.

She took all of him in her mouth, laving him with her tongue as she felt him begin to harden. His moan had her looking up his body to see sleepy eyes staring back at her, and she smiled around the flesh in her mouth.

LILIANA HART

"I thought I was having a really good dream," he said, bringing his arms up so his hands grasped the back of the chair.

"A really good reality," she said between licks, swirling her tongue around the plump head and feeling him jerk in her hand.

"You know what would make it better?"

"If you invited Juan Pablo the pool boy to join us?" she asked cheekily.

He arched a brow at that and gave her a look she knew meant retribution in her favorite form. "No. Not Juan Pablo. I was going to say it would be better if you swiveled around here and put that sweet pussy on my mouth."

Her hand flexed around the thick stalk of his cock and she gave a last satisfying lick before standing up. "Why didn't you say so?" She turned and lowered herself over his face, and then moaned as his hands gripped her hips and his tongue licked into her.

His cock waved like a flag in front of her face and she leaned back down to take it into her mouth, swallowing him down until he hit the back of her throat. And then she clamped her lips tightly and made swallowing motions until his hips jerked in short thrusts against her.

His moan vibrated against her clit and Audrey rode against his face and tongue, searching for the magic spot that would bring her complete ecstasy. His fingers skimmed across the open slit and she cried out as they slid smoothly inside her. Her hips moved up and down while her mouth continued to stroke his cock. She tasted the saltiness of his pre-cum and swirled her tongue over the sensitive head, knowing she could make him come without too much effort.

But she froze over him, her muscles going rigid, as he removed the finger from her vagina and trailed it to her back opening, massaging the tight hole before slipping just the tip of his finger inside.

"Relax," he whispered against her. "Just feel."

She closed her eyes and breathed in deeply, letting her muscles relax and doing as he asked. He pushed in further and she moaned at the incredible sensation as he touched nerve endings that had her pussy creaming.

"I want to take you here," he said, his tongue flicking once more across her clitoris, making her shudder. He stretched her wider, joining a second finger with the first, preparing her for something larger. "Can you imagine what it would feel like to have my cock fill you? To pump into you over and over again until you're coming around me?"

This was something she wanted to give him. Something she'd been prepared to offer. She lifted herself from his face and moaned as his fingers slipped out of her back channel. And then dug around in the pocket of her cover-up and pulled out the bottle of lube she'd found in his bedside drawer.

"What was it you said you'd do to me if you ever got me on my hands and knees?" she asked, tossing him the bottle.

He groaned and she swore his dick grew even larger at the thought. "Jesus, you'll have me coming in my hand," he said, squeezing the base of his cock as he got up from the lounger. "Are you sure?"

She loved that he'd ask, that he'd make sure it was what she really wanted. Instead of answering she moved into position on the lounger, propping herself up with her elbows as she spread her knees apart slightly.

"Fucking beautiful," he whispered, kneeling behind her. She didn't think about the scars, and she knew he didn't see them. The desire and love in his eyes told her he believed exactly what he said.

He leaned down and kissed the base of her

spine, and then he took her hips on either side and lined his cock up with her pussy, pushing in slowly so she felt every delicious inch of him as he stretched her. And then he began to move and she shattered into a million pieces.

Her head dropped down as he rode her hard and fast, barely giving her time to catch her breath as he pummeled inside her. The sensations built quickly, so she was just on the precipice of the orgasm of a lifetime. And then he stopped just as suddenly as he'd started and she whimpered in protest as he pulled out of her clutching body.

"Don't stop," she begged. "Don't leave me."

"I won't, sweetheart," he promised. "Not ever."

He grasped for the lube he'd laid on the lounger and she felt the cool gel against her flesh as he massaged it into her rear passage. She was so close to coming she was near tears, and every touch of his finger as it pushed the lube inside made the sensations of pleasure almost unbearable.

"Easy," he said, soothing her as if she were a mare ready to be mounted. She quivered beneath him as he pressed against the tiny rosette. "Breathe out and relax when I push in," he said, skimming his hands down her sides until he gripped her hips.

He pushed his way inside her and she breathed out as he'd told her, relaxing as he breached the muscle and the head of his cock was finally lodged inside her. She felt stretched as far as she could go, and she wondered how the rest of him would fit. Her skin was damp with sweat and her juices coated her thighs, and she needed a fucking orgasm more than she needed to breathe.

After a moment, she no longer felt the stretching muscles. She only felt her nerve endings tingle. Audrey pushed back against him slowly and he groaned as his cock slowly buried itself inside of her. She looked over her shoulder to see a look of fierce concentration on his face and sweat dripping from his brow.

"Take me," she told him, not wanting him to hold back. "Take all of me, Archer. I'm yours. Completely."

He broke under the spell of her words and he pushed the rest of the way inside her in one smooth stroke. And then she held onto the lounger for the ride as he gripped her hips and fucked her ass with a single-minded determination to claim what was his.

Her eyes went blurry as sensations piled on top of each other so she couldn't tell where one began and the next ended. Her muscles clamped around his cock and her pussy wept as she felt herself falling into oblivion. And then his hand reached around and pressed on her clit and she exploded.

Blackness closed in as she dropped to the lounger, and she felt him stiffen behind her and call out her name just before she felt the hot jets of his semen pulse inside her. He dropped down over her, his lips kissing the base of her neck, but she was too weak to do anything except focus on bringing oxygen to her lungs.

"Love you," he managed to get out. "And thank you for giving me your trust."

She rubbed his arm soothingly as she felt him soften and pull from her body, and he curled around her, his bigger frame cuddling hers.

"I love you too. I figured if I can trust you to get me out of the hell that was The End of the World, then a little kinky sex should be a piece of cake."

His body shook with laughter and his arms tightened around her waist. "You're a hell of a partner, Audrey Sharpe. But you haven't even begun to see my idea of a little kinky sex. I promise to show you everything I know if you'll marry me."

"How's a girl supposed to turn down a deal like that?" She smiled and let her eyes close as the sun beat down on their naked bodies. "Let's do it tomorrow. I don't think my legs will work until then."

"Good idea."

And they both drifted to sleep holding on to each other and the promise of a future together.

EPILOGUE

She'd left.

Shane should have felt relief that he'd finally pushed Doctor Shaw past the breaking point. But it only made him hate himself more.

He was a man who'd always had a purpose in life—a position. He'd been the youngest of "those MacKenzie kids," which was what everyone in town had called them when they'd been growing up. He'd milked it for all it was worth, as anyone with three older brothers and four older cousins would have done if they'd been in his position. But he'd never been an individual in a family of that size. Always grouped in with the others.

He hadn't become his own person until he'd

joined the Navy. And he hadn't discovered the type of man he was until he'd suffered through hell week and BUD/S. He'd found his niche there, and he'd eventually become a commander of those men. His purpose had been definitive at that point, and he'd lived for the next assignment and the thrill of doing a job that very few people in the world could do.

And now he had nothing. He *was* nothing. Because his career had defined him as a man, and he was discovering that maybe he wasn't quite the man he thought he was. He sure as hell didn't like the man he'd been living with the past weeks.

He sat on the edge of his bed and stared at the bottle of whiskey. It was already three quarters of the way gone. The bottle of Percocet sat next to him, mocking him as the pain from his injuries wracked his body.

Shaw had told him to fight through the pain. To wait past the point of when he thought he needed the pills before he took them, just so he knew he could. So he didn't rely on the hazy illusion of being pain-free. His good leg throbbed unmercifully and the stub of what was left of his other leg hurt more than it had a right to, considering there wasn't anything there to hurt.

Maybe he'd run his course in life. Maybe he'd done exactly what he was supposed to for the time he'd be able. It had been a good life. A worthy life. But he didn't feel like fighting through the pain. And in his wildest dreams, he couldn't imagine what worth there was in the rest of his life.

He should have felt *something*—fear maybe. Definitely anger. But even that emotion was numbed to nothing.

Shane unscrewed the cap on the whiskey and poured the remainder in a tumbler so it filled to the rim. And then he opened the bottle of pills and poured them all out into his hand. He was about to find out what kind of man he really was.

ABOUT THE AUTHOR

Liliana Hart is a *New York Times* and *USA Today* Bestselling Author in both the mystery and romance genres. After starting her first novel her freshman year of college, she immediately became addicted to writing and knew she'd found what she was meant to do with her life. She has no idea why she majored in music.

Liliana is an avid reader and a believer in all things romance. Her books are filled with witty dialogue, steamy sex, and the all-important happily-ever-afters her romantic soul craves. Since self-publishing in June of 2011, she's sold more than 1.2 million ebooks all over the world.

MY OTHER BOOKS

The MacKenzie Family Series

Dane

A Christmas Wish: Dane

Thomas

To Catch A Cupid: Thomas

Riley

Fireworks: Riley (Coming July 1, 2014)

Cooper

1001 Dark Nights: Captured in Surrender (Coming
March 11, 2014)

A MacKenzie Christmas

MacKenzie Box Set (includes the 5 books listed above)

Cade

Shadows and Silk

Secrets and Satin

Sins and Scarlet Lace

The MacKenzie Security Series (includes the 3 books
listed above)

Sizzle

Crave (Coming May 27, 2014)

The Collective Series

Kill Shot

The Rena Drake Series

Breath of Fire

Addison Holmes Mysteries

Whiskey Rebellion
Whiskey Sour
Whiskey For Breakfast
Whiskey, You're The Devil (Coming August 5, 2014)

JJ Graves Mysteries

Dirty Little Secrets
A Dirty Shame
Dirty Rotten Scoundrel
Down and Dirty (Coming November 25, 2014)

Standalone Novels/Novellas

All About Eve
Paradise Disguised
Catch Me If You Can
Who's Riding Red?
Goldilocks and the Three Behrs
Strangers in the Night
Naughty or Nice